Disney

THE LITTLE MERMAID

GUIDE TO MERFOLK

By ERIC GERON

Illustrated by ARIANNA REA, DENISE SHIMABUKURO, and MAX NARCISO

Property of Prince Eric

Disney PRESS

LOS ANGELES • NEW YORK

To my mother
—E.G.

Printed in the United States of America

First Hardcover Edition, April 2023

FAC-067395-23055

1 3 5 7 9 10 8 6 4 2

Library of Congress Control Number: 2022941368

ISBN 978-1-368-08040-8

Designed by Gegham Vardanyan

Visit disneybooks.com

SUSTAINABLE FORESTRY INITIATIVE Certified Sourcing
www.forests.org
SFI-01681
Logo Applies to Text Stock Only

CONTENTS

While I'm a prince
and next in line for the
throne, I'm also a sailor with
a fine ship and crew, and I'm most
at home out on the bottomless blue.
But lately, Mother has me on a "no
voyages" stint of staying in the castle.
She also strongly encouraged me to
read this book to better understand the
"perils" of merfolk—likely to instill fear
in me. She's always rattling on about
how their undersea world is pure evil, but
I'm not so sure. . . .

INTRODUCTION TO MERFOLK

Ah, the feared and reviled merfolk.

Welcome, dear reader. Within this book, I have compiled my findings from traveling the Seven Seas. Specifically, my findings on merfolk: half creature, half human. Beings of legend and lore, of brine and rippling kelp, of foam-capped waves, of undersea grotto and grove. We humans have always been fascinated by tales of mermaids, mermen, and merpeople. Most of us believe that merfolk exist even if we aren't among the lucky few who have seen them, but up until now, information about merfolk has been limited.

Through my discoveries from one coast to another—including tales told at tavern, in shanty, and on ship—this book aims to shed light on the many legends and lore surrounding merfolk and their happenings. Some people, including Her Majesty Queen Selina, would say that merpeople are more creature than human—and dangerous creatures at that. Read my field notes, dear reader, to decide for yourself.

THE
LURE
OF
MERFOLK

I have not been alone when it comes to my keen interest in the sea-dwellers. From the earliest days of yore to the present moment of the modern age, many have echoed my own obsession with merfolk, as seen in artwork and texts from around the world.

In this first section, I look at early records of merfolk's existence and how depictions of these creatures have made their way into our art and history, starting with mermaid sightings.

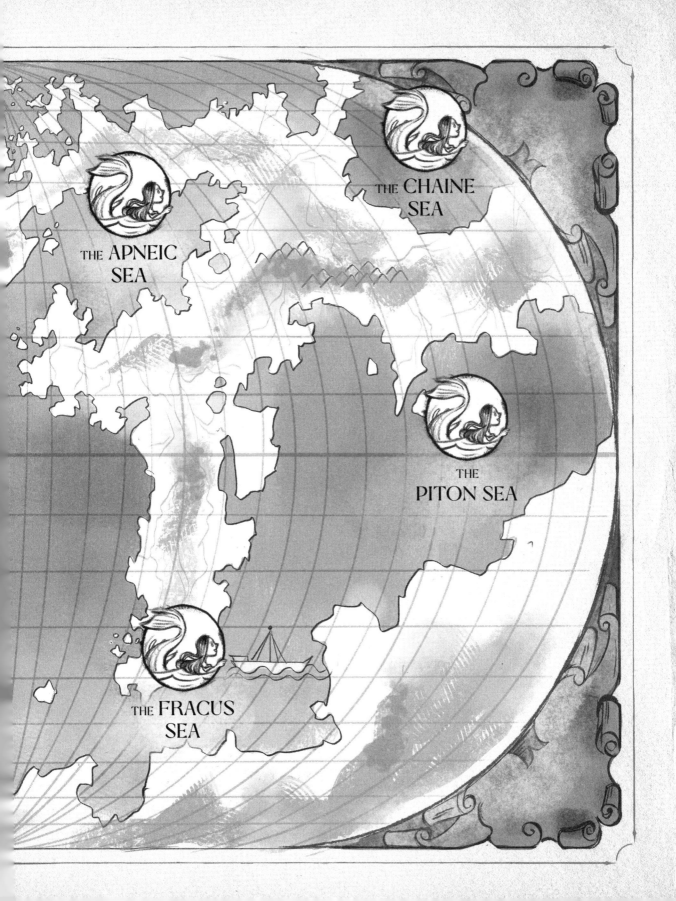

MERFOLK SIGHTINGS: COMPILED HISTORY

Well then. This should be good.

People from around the globe have recorded spotting merpeople throughout history. Basking in the sun on docks and jetties. Leaping in the waves. Splashing in the shallows. Diving to the deep.

I have taken the time to mark down on the previous map some of the many places where reports of merfolk sightings have been made, to further demonstrate the age-old awareness of the existence of merpeople and the rumors surrounding them over the years.

THE SAITHE SEA—1010

—A group of Saithe settlers fishing from the shore reported seeing a pale woman with green hair resting on a nearby ice floe. As a cloud moved to let the moon shine, she slid off into the icy waters, the last thing the settlers saw being the wide-fluked tail of a beluga. There have also been sightings of a sea witch with black octopus-like tentacles in place of legs.

THE APNEIC SEA—1339

—A medieval text characterizes what are undeniably merfolk: "from the navel up, the human form; from the navel down, the tail of a massive and colourful fish." These merfolk, as chronicled by the scribe, devoured the crews of ships sailing in the saline waters.

Is that what the scribe claimed?

THE CHAINE SEA—1405

—According to the inscription on a stone tablet, a Chaine fleet admiral navigating his treasure ship heard a mournful cry rise up from the rocks. Upon steering closer, he came upon a mermaid crying and shedding tears of pearls as she wove a cloth of intricate fibers.

My shipmates Hawkins, Mulligan, and Jerry think mermaids are too heartless to cry.

THE CARINAE SEA—1493—A fisherman

exploring the islands noted in his logbook that a woman swam up alongside his boat with bright eyes and fierce expression, a crown upon her head. After the fisherman called his sailors over to bear witness, she dove swiftly away, revealing "the scaly tail of an anaconda." Soon after, the entire boat was capsized, and the men swam to shore in a cold panic.

This sea is in my front yard, and I've never seen a mermaid. Neither has Joshua, the old fisherman here. At least not that he's admitted to me . . .

THE PITON SEA—1521—A Pitonian

expedition noted seeing a handsome man with the tail of a dolphin swimming through the straits, or else sitting combing his hair "as green as summer" and singing a song "as sweet as honey." A cosmographer strayed from the ship late one night, claiming, in a voice most vacant, to the captain at the wheel that she had to find the man whose voice beckoned her. She dove from the port side of the ship. She was never seen again.

THE FRACUS SEA—1545—In his

manuscript detailing currents and winds, a navigator from Port Galu recounts catching sight of a mermaid, reporting gazing down through the clear blue water and seeing "a human form with rounded tail, gliding along seagrass floor, with long hair undulating."

Sounds like a manatee mistaken for a mermaid.

THE BRINEDIVE SEA—1730—A

detailed map by an Ottillion cartographer illustrates a fishlike woman sitting above the waves, with accompanying translation stating, "Mermaids seen here."

I can't explain it, but I feel there's something out there in the ocean calling to me—I used to think it was the call of adventure and spirit of possibility, but maybe it's something else. Maybe it's a merperson.

Better not let Grimsby, my royal advisor, know any of this. He, like most people I know, finds merfolk villainous.

DEPICTIONS
OF MERFOLK

Not only have written records of merfolk sightings been noted around the world throughout history, but representations of these creatures have also made their way into the art and architecture of many civilizations. Below, you can see a timeline of merfolk depicted by people from various locations.

I've collected a lot of stuff from my voyages, including a jade mermaid figurine. I'm fascinated by merfolk, and dubious that they are foul.

← PORT GALU, 1150 →

← FROINCHES, 1478 →

— LENDENPOT. 1605 —

— OTRAX. 1868 —

Although these curious depictions of merfolk each look drastically different from one another, whether etched on church columns and reliefs, or included in medieval bestiaries, one thing remains true: humans through time have been intrigued by merfolk, and have included them in their art and culture, disparate civilizations united in this portrayal, generation after generation, from sea to sea.

Like these societies, I too craved to know more about merfolk and their mysterious watery realm.

Same here!

RELICS AND ARTIFACTS

Curios and keepsakes from around the world also work to support my commentary: humans have always felt a connection to merfolk. Below are a few objects that I have had the opportunity to personally inspect.

Our castle library's so packed with my curios and keepsakes I'm nearly out of room!

I have one like this that I found myself when diving for oysters! Isn't she beautiful? My little mermaid . . .

Human Face

Curved Fish Tail

When I was younger, I swear I saw something out there beyond the castle cliffs, frolicking in the tumbling waves. Maybe it was just a trick of the light.

JADE MERMAID

Jade is a stone said to bring luck and protection to its possessor.

Many believe that witnessing the flicker of a mermaid tail by the glow of the moon or the shimmer of mermaid scales by the light of the sun also brings about a fruitful future for the beholder.

Origin: **Coast of Catgenuie**

Date: *1888*

SAPPHIRE MERMAID RING

The pale blue "mermaid sapphire" set into this ring is a symbol for repairing rifts and creating harmony. It represents an age-old ideal of prosperity and peace between humans and merfolk.

Legend has it that some humans can gaze into mermaid sapphires to see into their undersea realm.

Origin: **Coast of Maquinto**

Date: **1864**

BRONZE MERMAN

Bronze is said to bring about strength and stability.

This bronze merman figurine was recovered from a sunken Otraxian ship off the coast of Cropenhügen. Notice its similarity to the jade mermaid from the distant Carinae waters. Coincidence?

Origin: **Coast of Cropenhügen**

Date: **1879**

More pearls of wisdom . . .

PEARL MERMAID PENDANT

Set in gold fashioned in the form of a mermaid, this pearl pendant is said to spell misfortune for its wearer. The lustrous gem of the sea with its unmatched iridescence is also a mark of wealth. How can something so luminous! so divine! so effervescent! be born and borne away—plucked from the dark, dull bed and briny, barnacled husk of the mollusk? I digress. . . .

Some cultures postulate that pearls are created from the tears of mermaids, but that has yet to be properly documented.

Origin: **Coast of Rázil**

Date: **1863**

THE MERFOLK FASCINATION WITH HUMANS

While history has always shown humans' fascination with merfolk, it was not until recently that I made a discovery that led me to believe that this fascination may run both ways.

During an early voyage of mine while researching for this book, I decided to take a swim off the side of the ship in a location infamous for merfolk sightings. After diving headlong into the refreshing Carinae waters, a sparkle in the white sand below caught my eye. I dove down further, happening upon the most peculiar formation: a grotto full of human trinkets, stashed neatly on shelves of rock . . . dare I say, organized. It would have been impossible for a human to arrange so many objects so far from the surface. In my opinion, a merperson must have been responsible!

Back aboard the ship, I was dripping wet and bursting with excitement, but after telling my crewmates of my most miraculous discovery, I could no longer pinpoint the grotto's location. Slipping back into the ocean in a disorienting churn of bubbles, I scoured the seafloor.

It was gone. Perhaps the ship had drifted. But the memory remains even now, emblazoned in my mind.

THE MERFOLK'S COLLECTION

ON THESE PAGES ARE SOME OF THE DOODADS I RECALL
SEEING IN THAT CLUTTERED GROTTO.

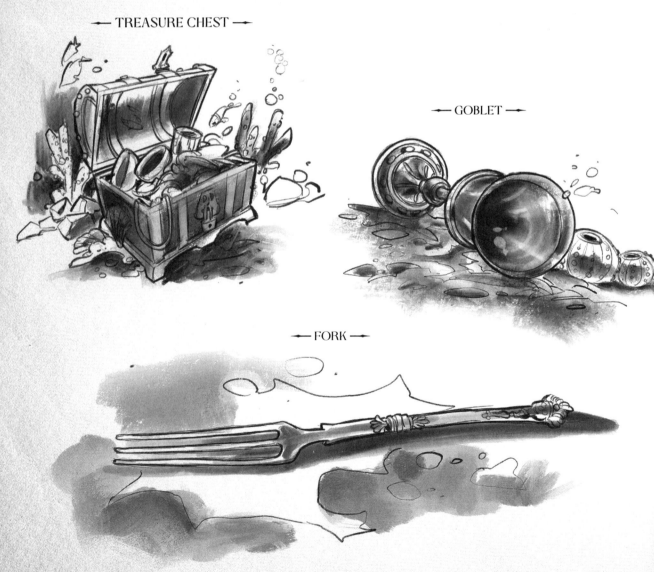

— TREASURE CHEST —

— GOBLET —

— FORK —

— GOLD SPYGLASS —

— CANDELABRA —

What could a merperson possibly be doing collecting all these mostly worthless keepsakes?

Perhaps the merfolk were as curious about life above as humans like myself were about life below. And perhaps whatever falls into the sea from above is no longer ours. Thus continued an unwavering pursuit of knowledge about merfolk through my various voyages.

For all the bad things Mother says about merpeople,
I'm willing to wager that evil doesn't go around hoarding forks. . . .

HISTORY
OF
MERFOLK

Merpeople have coexisted with humans for as long as anyone can remember, with humans both drawn to merfolk mystique and afraid of the threat they may pose to our livelihood.

In my investigation, I sought to uncover whether this divide between human and merperson has always been. In the pages that follow, I try to explain our complicated history with merfolk and how we have gotten to the strained coexistence we face today.

Max! Bad dog! What was he doing licking my book? Rosa, our other housekeeper here, just fed him. I guess he really likes the taste of books.

It's all right. I can never stay mad at Max for long. He's my best friend!

THE TIME BEFORE

One of my voyages led me into an ancient cave off the coast of Nevezuela, where age-old glyphs illustrated a time when there was peace and harmony between humans and merpeople. These pictures detailed humans respecting those inhabiting bodies of water, and merfolk admiring those lodging on land and loam.

According to those petroglyphs, merpeople honored the earth, humans, and the ocean. The images on the cave walls showed rulers of land and rulers of sea meeting at the shore, trading resources and learning to speak in the others' tongue. Shells and sea flowers for tree branches and textiles. Boats out on the water, guided and helped along by merfolk with fair winds and tranquil waters. Merpeople and humans lazing on rocks under the warm sun, or swimming together in groups. These images indicate that there was a period of time when humans and merfolk were friendly, perhaps even friends.

If there was once harmony, what happened?

THE ANCIENT DIVISION

But clearly, that accord between human and merperson was not meant to last, as we do not see merfolk eagerly interacting with humans today. To help give us an indicator of why this may be the case, I have translated the archaic letters accompanying petroglyphs in the sea cave. I imagine that, just like us humans, the merfolk would gather and recite these old words to one another as a way to connect to their past.

Oh, this old lore . . . but what does it mean?

ALONG THE ROCKY COAST OF PARADISE,

WHERE THE TIDE BRINGS SEA TO LAND,

TWO RULERS DREW LINES IN THE SAND.

GUIDED BY ANCIENT FEARS, THEY KEPT THEIR REALMS

DIVIDED, BORDERED BY THE SAME CHURNING SURF,

YET WORLDS APART . . .

UNTIL A STORM CAST THEIR CHILDREN ASHORE

TOGETHER, MERMAID AND MAN, SIDE BY SIDE . . .

AND LOVE TURNED THE TIDE.

THE FATEFUL RIFT

Why did the ruler of each realm decide to construct borders and boundaries? What were these ancient fears guiding humans and merfolk to sever ties? Rumors speak of how the Sea King grew angry at boats choking the surface, nets trawling and catching fish and other beloved companions to merfolk, and rubbish falling into and sullying sacred and once-pure waters. Tales also speak of how merfolk betrayed humans by capsizing their boats and summoning sharks, rays, and jellyfish—along with treacherous sailing weather—to chase humans out of their sea domain.

Regardless of the reason for the divide between merfolk and humans, we do know that we must stay vigilant of merfolk and their trickery, and what better way to do so than to understand who and what these creatures are?

Mother lives in constant fear and isolation. Father did too when he was still alive. That's why our kingdom's been cut off from the rest of the world for so long. But I don't want to be like my parents in that way. I want to stay open to what's out there. It's the only way our islands can thrive and grow.

PART
OF
THEIR
WORLD

It is prudent that I make no assumptions about your preexisting knowledge concerning merfolk, so I utilize these next few pages to illustrate their physicality, their anatomy, and the keen difference between the "merperson" and the "singing merperson," otherwise known as the "siren." This next section will tell you everything you need to know about merfolk and their abilities.

What I'd give to see a real-life merperson! A siren . . . not so much.

THE MERPERSON

WHAT IS A MERPERSON?

A merperson is half fish, half human. I believe that the species of fish for the tail may vary, as reports have shown a wide array of tails: fluked, flat and paddle-like, diaphanous, bulbous, and other diversifications.

Perhaps this variety of fins is a direct result of their immediate environments?

I have never been able to get a close enough look at a merperson to truly sketch an accurate drawing, but from what I've gathered through testimonies and transcripts, it seems these images may provide a starting place for us to begin imagining the kinds of merfolk out there.

The merperson breathes underwater and cannot likely survive for much time out of the water.

⟶ THE MERMAID ANATOMY ⟵

Cranium

Mandible

Ribs

Caudal Fin

Pelvic Fin

Merpeople are known for using their
strong tails to propel themselves through the water.
Diurnal? Nocturnal? Crepuscular?

This seems pretty accurate, from what I've heard.

— THE MERMAN ANATOMY —

Pinnae

Merpeople are likely cold-blooded, allowing them to comfortably live in icy water.

Cranial Fins

Brachial & Cubital Fins

Caudal Banding

Cycloid Scales on Tail

Gills?

Spiny Ridge

— JUVENILE MERFOLK ANATOMY —

Tiny Tails

Torso

Little Hands

When born, merfolk hatchlings may resemble infant humans with legs fused in piscine form.

MERPEOPLE CANNOT CRY

During one expedition, I came upon a decades-old tale about a fisherman who claimed to have seen a mermaid with his own eyes. The story says he was out dragging his nets in the bay when a beautiful face broke through the surface without so much as a ripple. She spoke to him, sharing that her child had been taken from her by a shiver of sharks. When asked why she shed no tears, she admitted that merpeople cannot cry. The fisherman was quick to insult her, calling her cruel, callous, and cold, which sent the mermaid diving off in hurt and loathing. If the story is true, my belief is that the fisherman misunderstood her hurt.

I suppose they must
feel emotions that much
more deeply. . . .

THE SINGING SIREN

While the general anatomy and abilities of merfolk are widely agreed upon, there are some rumors of merpeople with special gifts. Those with the gift of song are referred to as sirens.

Rumors say the siren often first appears as the benign flick of a tail signaling a sprightly hello in the rolling waves. Innocent. Playful. Jocund. But they are known to enchant humans by using their melismatic voices to bewitch and ensnare, to capture and devour, to lure to a watery grave.

Not this again. I don't believe this lore about mermaids luring sailors to their deaths.

I often hear my mates talk about the sirens, saying not even the strongest can resist their sweet songs.

That's Hawkins and Mulligan for you. Fearing the worst. Less gabbing and more running rigging, in my opinion.

THE SWAY OF SIRENS

I was bent on hearing the ill-fated music of the siren, despite the warnings.

In the port of the main Maquintian village, the busiest in the region, I met an old woman who spoke of the songs heard drifting inland from a distant arch of limestone every night of the full moon. She spoke of a rowboat full of men who had sailed out to it, but only one made it back to shore, screaming that it had been surrounded by singing sirens who had taken them below the water.

At dusk, when every door was bolted and locked, and the full moon rose in a starry sky, I tied myself to a fountain in the square and waited. Eventually, I heard something. A pure song, floating in from the sea on a salty breeze. The sound was intoxicating, beckoning me. Luckily, the sturdy rope held, despite my attempts to struggle free and sprint headlong into the sea.

Come the morning, I had a friend release me from the rope. I rubbed my wrists and stared out at the arch. The miry fog in my mind slowly cleared, replaced by the reality of what had transpired.

The siren tale was true. I set out to gather more accounts of the sirens and their potent songs. . . .

SIREN SONGS

Does every siren song entice? Are there different types of songs, and abilities within them?

I wrote down the nursery rhymes recited by those in the sundry port towns I passed through. I strongly believe these nursery rhymes reflect the different types of siren songs that may exist. . . .

These songs may each achieve a different outcome, as described below:

— LURE SONG —

A tempestuous trance disguised as a tune
Invites bewitched sailors to meet their doom—
Jaunty ditty, a lullaby in verse,
An ill fate to those who nourish the curse.

I absolutely don't believe merfolk could be this treacherous. But looks like I may invest in wax ear plugs . . . for the crew.

Just in case.

— HEART SONG —

An aria sweet as honey dripping
Sends cool hearts aflame and senses slipping—
Lulling the longing to wander and stray,
Following the ballad into the spray.

Yeah, this would never work on me. Not in a million years.

— SICK SONG —

A powerful spell from sibilant lips
Sours sailor stomachs on seaward trips—
Vomiting bile, to retch and to heave,
From the sorcery this siren does weave.

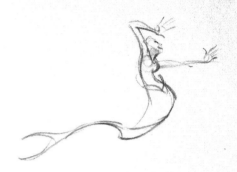

This sounds rough. I wouldn't like to experience it.

— DREAM SONG —

A choral din on endless waves sweeping
Sends favorable winds for calm sleeping—
Calming hymn to guide like the placid bream,
Night after night with the unyielding dream.

— HEAL SONG —

A potent siren tune more sharp than flat
Mends bruised wounds from scraps and bites from the bat—
Fighting poison to cleanse and to discard,
Restoring health through the melodic bard.

Hey! I wouldn't mind this song one bit.

— SHARK SONG —

A canorous chant charms the gentle breeze,
Calling forth dangerous ocean beasts with ease—
Summoning keen sharks to bite and to snap.
Giant jaws remove sailors from the map.

— LUCK SONG —

A tumult in the surf with spirant sound,
Kismet kisses routes with good fortune abound—
Lauding riches, to happiness and health,
The operatic chorus bestows wealth.

Ahh . . . music to my ears. Forget our mermaid figurehead! If we could travel alongside this siren, it would be smooth sailing!

— WRECK SONG —

A cacophonous chorus of shrill cries
Cracks the mainmast like lightning from the skies—
Snapping boom and bowsprit like twigs and sticks,
The cursed refrain rife with destructive tricks.

I'm not buying it. . . . All this chaos from a song?!

I've sailed the seas for weeks at a time, chasing Panishian galleons, the works, and I have never heard a single siren song! Maybe it's fate. Or maybe I'm not paying close enough attention, like Grimsby is always chiding me about.

COMPANIONS
OF
MERFOLK

The marine environs are home not just to sirens and merfolk, but to the creatures with whom they coexist. . . .

Much as the witch has a familiar, according to legends, each merperson has a creature who assists in their journey of life. This marine creature can be anything from a crab or fish to a dolphin or whale. Over the next few pages, I explain the different layers of the sea, the many inhabitants thereof, and how they live together.

If I had it my way, I'd see less sea creatures and more merpeople!
Who am I kidding—sea creatures are pretty great, too.

SEA LEVELS

Before learning about the animal companions of merfolk, it is important to know the distinction between the different ocean layers, as well as the various sea creatures that naturally dwell within each. Such findings were documented in the logbook of a submersible captain who is a friend of mine.

SUNLIGHT LAYER

TWILIGHT LAYER*

MIDNIGHT LAYER

ABYSS

TRENCHES

*Merpeople and sirens likely found dwelling here

CREATURES OF THE SUNLIGHT LAYER

The sunlight layer is the topmost level of the sea, warm to the touch and clear to the eye. Certain sea creatures inhabit or visit this sunny, lilting part of the ocean near the surface....

CORAL REEFS & SECRET LAGOONS

The coral reefs and seaside lagoons teem with vibrancy and life.

Sometimes I ask Grimsby to ready the horse and carriage so I can visit the beautiful lagoon with a little waterfall in the rain forest on our island.

POWDER BLUE TANG

Bright yellow tropical fish with vibrant blue stripes that lives off algae in reef flats

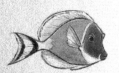

I see this little guy out there all the time!

SEAHORSE

A small fish with the head of a horse, a body of bony armor, and a curled tail for anchoring

GANNET

A white seabird that plunge-dives from the sky to catch fish in the watery depths

Or in fisherman Joshua's case, to steal the fish right off the deck of his boat!

CHRISTMAS TREE WORM

A sea worm with a tube-shaped body and crown of ruffled, feather-like plumage

RIBBON EEL

An eel with a long thin body, wide-open jaws, and prominent dorsal fins

I tend to avoid anything with wide-open jaws.

FEATHER STAR

A plant-like creature with many feathery arms that allow it to attach to surfaces or billow onward

MOON JELLYFISH

Ghostlike jellyfish with see-through bells and pale tentacles

FLATWORM

Brightly colored sea worm that hides in cracks of coral or flutters through the open waters

I've seen these whenever I take a dip!

LIMPET

A cone-shaped sea snail often found clinging to rocks

CREATURES OF THE TWILIGHT LAYER

The twilight layer is the second-topmost level of the sea, a bit dimmer and colder than the sunlight layer. Some sea creatures gravitate primarily to this oceanic level. . . .

MERMAN'S REEF

In deeper and darker waters, Merman's Reef is a place where shipwrecked things such as barrels, sails, masts, and nets accumulate. Such activity draws a host of sea creatures and merfolk.

STURGEON

A long, large scaleless fish with a sharklike fin and bony plates covering its entire body

BLANKET OCTOPUS

An octopus with sheets of webbing stretching between some of its arms

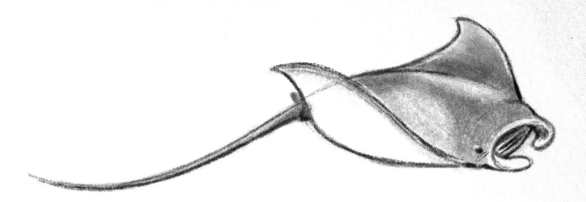

MANTA RAY

A large ray with gill slits, angular fins, a thin tail, and an eye on either side of its body

MORAY EEL

A snakelike fish with a ribbonlike fin running across the top of its elongated body

MIMIC OCTOPUS

An octopus that can change color to disguise itself as other sea creatures

PUFFERFISH

A fish with prickly skin that can inflate into a sphere to scare off threats

Love these little guys!

CREATURES OF THE MIDNIGHT LAYER

The midnight layer is the third-topmost level of the sea, darker and colder still, attracting the likes of a new gathering of sea creatures who embrace the chilly depths. . . .

SHIPWRECK GRAVEYARD

Deeper in the sea there lies a landscape of ruined ships, sunken galleons with lavish dining rooms destroyed, chipped china plates, shattered bay windows, rusted silverware, and cracked mirrors. Ships piled atop one another, perched on craggy rocks . . .

I'm fortunate to not be intimately acquainted with this place.

Perhaps these are the same ships from "The Tale of a Thousand and One Shipwrecks" on page 185.

FLYING GURNARD

A fish with large eyes and blue-tipped wings that skims the sand on the seafloor

BULLWHIP KELP

An algae seaweed that forms lush kelp forests after its holdfast attaches to bedrock below

BRITTLE STAR

A starfish-like creature that uses its spindly arms to creep across the seafloor

TIGER SHARKS

An aggressive shark with stripes running the length of its large gray body

No thank you!

CREATURES
OF THE ABYSS

The abyss is the penultimate level of the sea, steeped in shadows and home to the few sea creatures who shy away from the sunlight, but who also avoid the darkest of depths below. . . .

GIANT SQUID

A behemoth squid with eight arms, two tentacles, giant eyes, a parrotlike beak, and a pointy mantle

GIANT ISOPOD

A pale, louse-like creature of epic proportions with a protective shell, many legs, and antennae

BIOLUMINESCENT CLAM

Glowing clam that flashes bright colors in the darkness

COMB JELLY

A transparent tentacled mass that swims through the water

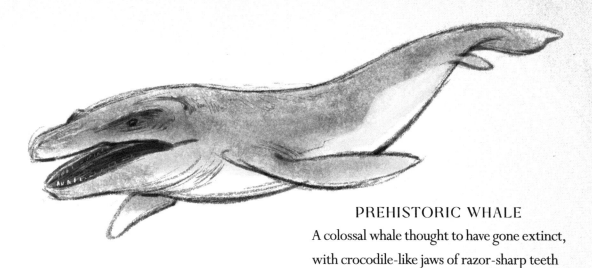

PREHISTORIC WHALE
A colossal whale thought to have gone extinct, with crocodile-like jaws of razor-sharp teeth

SEA DRAGON
A dragon that glides through the dark water with bioluminescence glowing in its veined wings

SNAIL & SLUG
One mollusk that crawls along with a shell, and another that exists without one

These sea creatures better stay down there. . . .

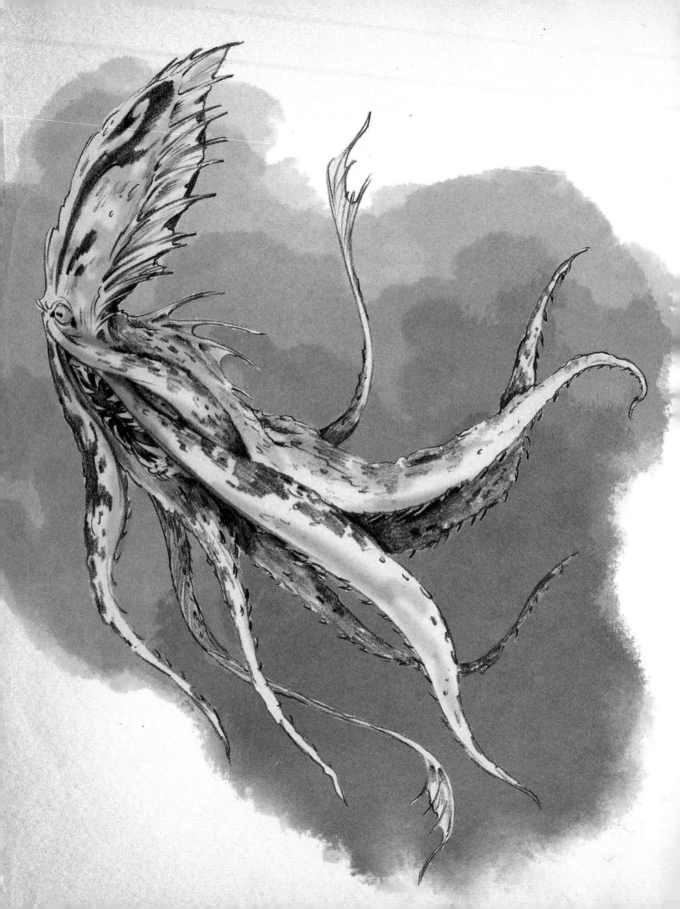

CREATURES OF THE TRENCH

Little is known about the darkest, deepest level of the sea: the trench. A bleak realm of complete and utter darkness and solitude, with few sea creatures able to survive the extremes...This alien depth is rumored to be full of terror in the pitch darkness punctuated by eerie flashes of light....

ANGLERFISH

A bony fish with a big mouth of sharp teeth and a glowing rod on its head to lure food

KRAKEN

A legendary sea monster akin to a monstrous squid with suckered arms

MOON RAY

A pure-white stingray with pink spots that looks like moonlight flying through the fathoms

BLOBFISH

A deep-sea fish that catches crabs and mollusks on the bottom of the ocean

MARIANA HYDRA

A prehistoric sea serpent that dwells in the crevices of rocks in the darkest parts of the sea

SHRIMP

A white, lobsterlike creature with a segmented abdomen, long whiskers, and beady eyes

GIANT TUBE WORM

A mammoth white tube worm with a red plume that grows on the deepest ocean floor

I'm comforted knowing how far down in the water this thing lives!

COMMON MERFOLK COMPANIONS

Max is my human companion.

Many stories claim that merfolk have the gift of gab in that they are able to <u>communicate with all sea creatures</u>, including their own guides, protectors, and confidantes. Each consort, comrade, or crony must be well suited for each individual merperson. Below, I describe some of the most common companions of merpeople as mentioned throughout various tales. . . .

I knew it!

FISH

The fish is a formidable friend to a merperson. Fish are quick and can easily keep up with a speedy merperson, are adept secret keepers, and can easily hide in a merperson's hair at a moment's notice. One downside of fish as friend is the risk of their being caught by humans.

CRAB

The crab is a loyal and kind companion. Crabs are sincere and care deeply for the well-being of the merperson, scuttling and swimming alongside them and issuing a wealth of sage advice. A downside is they are often anxious, irritable, and easily overwhelmed.

I've seen this served here at the castle on more than one occasion. . . .

TURTLE

The turtle is a trustworthy comrade. Turtles are particularly helpful at easing the worries of a fretful merperson with their calm and soothing presence. They make for excellent listeners. One drawback is that they sometimes have difficulty keeping up with a merperson's fast pace.

OTTER

The playful and frisky otter is not for the shy and timid merperson. Instead, otters are a good fit for a merperson who has just as much energy and zest for life. They enjoy cuddling and hand-holding and like to be cradled, requiring much attention and doting upon.

Another disadvantage to the otter, despite how cozy and fuzzy, is that they are awfully chatty and a bit reckless, pulling off pranks such as stealing precious shells and cracking them open with rocks at the surface.

If I were a merperson, I'd pick the otter. They sound fun!

SEA LION

The sea lion is a graceful and elegant counterpart to the merperson who enjoys frolicking in the waves, winding through streams of kelp, and basking on rocks in the hot sun. The merperson mustn't mind that the sea lion can at times be territorial of its rock. This also acts as an advantage for the merperson who values time spent alone, since the sea lion can break for air above on rock, dock, or secluded beach while the merperson chooses to stay in the water. Trouble may arise in that sea lions tend to attract sharks.

MANATEE

For the sluggish, meandering, leisurely merperson, the manatee makes a fine friend. The manatee cruises at a slow pace, munching seagrass or else lurking in the dripping quiet of mangrove forests. A merperson who matches with a manatee also enjoys a relaxed existence of repose.

DOLPHIN

The zipping, chirping dolphin is recommended for the most athletic of the merpeople, to breach, to porpoise, and to race alongside in the wake of ships. The dolphin is also the most talkative of sea creature companions, speaking often and quickly. A less athletic merperson can grab hold of their dorsal fin and let the dolphin assist them in their travels, especially long-distance treks.

Note: Rumored to pull the Sea King's royal chariot; for more on the Sea King, see page 80.

WHALE

For the merperson craving knowledge, worldly insight, and wisdom beyond their years, a whale to glide beside is a satisfactory choice. The whale is a most revered comrade for its unmatched size, slow and steady cadence, and serene demeanor, including the calming song it croons and the fizzing footprint it leaves on the surface. The whale acts as protector against threats and provides cover with its enormous barnacle-encrusted flanks. The merperson can also ride it.

*I suppose I spoke too soon.
I'd pick the whale.*

MERFOLK RITUALS

Now that I have shown the diverse array of animals cohabiting the waters with merfolk, it is time to dig into my belief that merpeople have various rituals and behaviors: a prescribed order, much like humans. Old legends suggest merpeople hold the moon sacred, as it controls the rise and fall of tides. Similarly, they hold the sun, stars, and natural world in high esteem, and engage in customs honoring them. Here, I provide theories and insights into the sacred merfolk rituals. . . .

Fascinating . . .

MERFOLK MOONS

Using the moonlight, merfolk infuse scale and fin with renewed energy and healing. Many scholars believe that, depending on the type of moon, merfolk can experience different effects. Below are some moons that I have heard rumors of during my travels.

CORAL MOON

A reddish moon said to bring good fortune to merfolk. When a Coral Moon fills the sky above, merfolk gather in groups to celebrate its presence for a single phase.

My crew's superstitious about this old lore. Not sure why, especially if it's just some sort of harmless gathering of merpeople. They claim it's when the Sea King calls his daughters to lure men to their deaths. It's ridiculous.

SPONGE MOON

A pale and porous-looking moon said to recharge the energies in reefs, resulting in renewed spirits amongst merfolk, who soak up its soft rays.

CARP MOON

This gray-faced moon imbues the beholder with strength, courage, and the will to persevere.

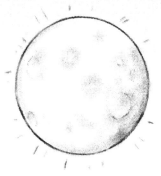

ANGLER MOON

A bright white moon unveils all paths and provides light in dark times, instilling trust in the inner trajectory and setting merfolk on a true and swift current.

CLAM MOON

Half of this moon is cloaked in shadow, signifying the halved nature of merpeople with part fish and part human. A wash of bronze from this moon fills one's life with blessings, abundance, and wholeness.

TROUT MOON

The moon cast in a rainbow aura promises to refill one's well of hope and intentions for a better life.

CHUB MOON

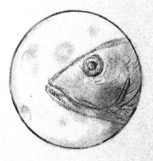

Silver blue, gleaming, and glimmering, this moon provides clarity about dreams, bolsters creativity, and mends breakdowns in communication.

Sometimes I like gazing out the north tower up at the moon, wondering what else is out there, beyond where the roaring waves meet the shore. . . .

MERFOLK SUNS

Basking in sunlit water, merfolk soak up heat to warm their fins, but the sun isn't just fruitful for bathing. Many wives' tales claim that the sun also provides different remedies for merfolk depending on where it is located in the sky. A rising sun, a setting sun, and a sun at its zenith all invoke different sorts of powers.

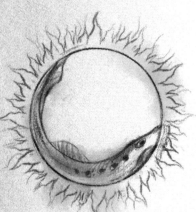

LAMPREY SUN

A fierce ball of fire drains negativity and soothes fears, and its blistering heat offers a sheath of protection from enemies.

SALMON SUN

This blazing sun brings about a renewal of spirit and abundance of tranquility.

RAY SUN

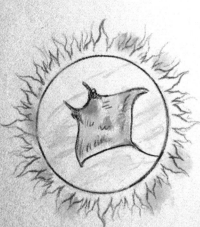

The flares dancing on this sun grant grace and clear currents of energy, allowing for refined focus and magnified clarity leading to the soul's true purpose.

STURGEON SUN

The blush of this sun encourages care of self and blesses the mind with wisdom.

SLUG SUN

The sparkle and glare of this sun endow the viewer with determination, patience, and perseverance.

SPRAT SUN

The shimmer and shine of this sun thaw fears and result in a relaxed state of being.

Grim should soak up plenty of this one's rays.

MERFOLK STARS

Stories say merpeople have a deep connection to the cosmos, and that includes constellations. It is said that merpeople, like humans, wish on stars and use them for navigating. Below are some constellations that I have heard referred to in stories about merfolk.

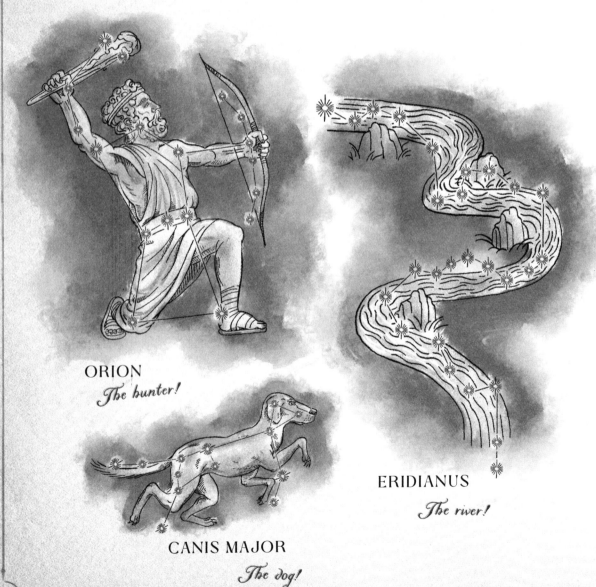

ORION
The hunter!

CANIS MAJOR
The dog!

ERIDIANUS
The river!

The fish!
PISCES

CASSIOPEIA

Sometimes we play a game on the ship to see who can be the first to spot these constellations.

GEMINI
The twins!

RITUALS FOR FINDING ONE'S VOICE

For merfolk, finding one's singing voice is a rite of passage, denoting a coming of age. The more they can achieve in the realm of musicality, the higher their status.

But how do they find and fine-tune their emerging vocal repertoires and ranges? A few theories I have stumbled across . . .

LOW-NOTE RITUAL

The way for a merperson to discover their lowest singing note is to swim to the deepest depth on the night of a low tide and to hear which sort of guttural grunt escapes their lips there.

HIGH-NOTE RITUAL

To pinpoint their highest note, a merperson breaks the surface and tries trilling at the frequency of a seagull. If they succeed, a dolphin breaches in an arc overhead, vocalizing at the same whistle-like

Always go out on a high note, I say!

frequency. The merpeople refer to the dolphin that materializes as a "Porpoise of Purpose."

MERFOLK-MESMERIZING RITUAL

An effective way to practice potent spells through song is by singing to fish and seeing if the desired result occurs. Sea creatures such as turtles and dolphins also make suitable test subjects.

BUBBLE-NOTE RITUAL

For more gifted vocalists, trapping musical notes in bubbles helps hone the craft. The bubbles hold individual notes for the merperson to listen back to and identify places for improvement.

Truly riveting.

BUBBLE-NET RITUAL

The hallmark of an experienced, fully mature merperson is the ability to conjure a bubble net, which corrals all the bubble-confined musical notes to generate a symphony of harmonic, or in some cases discordant, sounds. This ritual functions to fortify the vocal agility of the merperson.

MERFOLK OBJECTS AND ITEMS

From different accounts, I have hypothesized that merpeople use undersea objects for their various needs in ways that humans would never think to:

— seashell comb used for brushing hair

— basket stars for nets

— line of razor clam shells bound together into a fence

— coral used to make furniture

— polished shells used as roof tiles

— seashells to use like tools

Merfolk sound very resourceful.

— THE CONCH —

One object in particular comes up time after time in various stories of the sea: the conch. Merfolk can blow into the shell of a sea snail to summon others from near and far. The Sea King uses this to call his subjects, and his daughters can hear the shell's musical tone even from the farthest reaches of the Seven Seas. The instrument is also called the Seashell Horn, Shell Trumpet, Triton's Trombone, and Water Beacon.

Reminds me of the one I found here on the island. I should add it to my collection of keepsakes in our library if there's room.

CUSTOMS
OF
MERFOLK

Many legends claim that merpeople, like humans, have customs, traditions, superstitions, gatherings, and celebrations. Some say their values are benign, while others believe they spring from heinous intentions. Fear of the unknown seems to sink ships and set imaginations ablaze. There is so much more to know about the customs and cultures of others.

In the proceeding pages, I shall delve into such rumors of details swirling around daily life under the sea. . . .

One day, I want to tell Mother not to fear the unknown, but to embrace it.

SUPERSTITIONS OF MERFOLK

We shall begin by covering how merpeople are likely highly superstitious creatures. It is rumored that they put forth many practices to sway the outcome of an event for the better, and work to recognize and avoid omens that could spell calamitous futures.

GESTURES OF GOOD LUCK

Merfolk apparently tickle the feet of a paddling albatross for good tidings. They also knock on driftwood for good fortune and drop mollusks bearing black pearls into the abyss.

See that? We have way more in common than my crewmates believe!

TOKEN OF BAD LUCK

Merfolk swimming too close to a ship is said to bring bad luck.

It is also considered bad luck for a merperson to keep a human object in their dwelling.

I'm sure the Sea King doesn't like any merperson swimming near the surface, and I don't blame him! Still, I wish things were different. . . .

GATHERINGS AND CELEBRATIONS

As in human cultures, there is evidence in old books to suggest that merfolk celebrate various events, and gather to do so. Missing a gathering or celebration is a serious transgression within merpeople circles. Below are some common mermaid celebrations and gatherings:

BIRTHDAYS

Enrobed in singing cloaks of fizz, merfolk blow bubble rings at cakes made of sand.

BLUE HOLE

Every year, merfolk journey to the same location: a blue hole in the Chaine Sea, where they remain for sixteen days. Many merfolk bring along preserved tail scales of long-lost ancestors to toss into the sinkhole as they make wishes. On the way home, they search for a blue whale, hoping to touch its tail for good fortune and safe travel. Once the festivities have ended, they play makeshift drums to announce their return.

GIFT GIVING

Merpeople pass down family heirlooms such as jewels, pearls, sea fossils, instruments, and precious stones.

I wonder if Mother will ever give me anything of Great-Grandmother's. . . .

MERFOLK WEDDINGS

Merfolk get married, and on their wedding days, they plant coral in the ocean floor and throw a bouquet of coral into the blue. The merperson who catches it is fated to fall in love next. The betrothed wear coronets of kelp.

Lashana and Rosa are always asking me when I'm going to settle down with someone, but I'm all about getting out there and exploring the map!

MOLT OF SCALE AND SKIN

Twice a year, merfolk swim to the ocean floor and rub their tails against rocks to shed old scales. New scales regrow with twice the shine and luster of the molted scales.

MIGRATIONS AND MEALS

In many stories, merfolk enjoy a feast of seagrass called a Meal of Gratitude on sandbars on days of low tide. They are also known to consume clams during mid-autumn. Whether or not merpeople migrate and have specific feeding grounds is unknown, but I believe when they travel, they do so in pods. I would surmise that common merfolk meals typically comprise the following:

— *clams*   — *scallops*
— *deep-sea shrimp* — *sea cucumbers*
— *mussels*   — *seagrass*
— *oysters*   — *sea urchins*
— *periwinkles*   — *sea vegetables*
— *razor clams*   — *seaweeds*

AQUATIC SPORTS

Many along my journey have reported that merfolk entertain themselves by playing athletic games. These aquatic sports are said to be played on days of quietude and nights of calmness....

PUFFERBALL

Merfolk flick a puffer fish with their tails in a game of keep-away.

STONESWEEP

Merfolk use their tails to sweep a stone across the seafloor and into a crevasse.

SPEEDRACE

It is allegedly common for merfolk to race each other competitively.

Growing up, me and the servants would race each other in the castle halls.

SEA CHICKEN

Two merpeople dive into the pitch-black abyss of a trench. The first to pull up short loses.

SQUID RIDE

Rumors describe merfolk hitching rides on an unwitting giant squid for sport.

HOW MERFOLK BECOME RULERS

Let me guess: lots of boring rules of succession?
Or is that just a royal human thing?

As you will come to find in later sections, all merfolk are said to be governed by the Sea King, and distinct regions by his seven daughters. Because of this, there seems to be the notion that merfolk are made rulers through the royal bloodline. To date, the Sea King remains sovereign, and therefore each of his daughters is next in line to the Coral Throne, as well as ruler of her own waters in the meantime.

However, many stories indicate that there are also trainings and trials to prepare a mermaid princess to become a revered ruler. There are tales of tests of strength and dexterity, where each daughter had to perform an act of service to the seas, whether it was freeing a turtle from a fisherman's net or dragging debris of the human world out of the sea from the miry murk.

There may also be tests to ensure proper communication skills, whether through use of the conch for kingdom-to-kingdom contact, or through bubbles or schools of fish carrying words and messages on the shifting tides.

Tail-slapping seems to be an efficient form of communication to master. This enables a mermaid to warn her subjects that danger is near, spurring them to move away from the location.

A ruler must be decisive. To evince this trait, the daughters of the Sea King likely have to make swift decisions in the face of peril, with the outcome directly impacting their status.

Merfolk rulers must also have integrity, keeping to the laws of the water and never straying to the surface. They listen to their royal advisors, train in combat, and keep calm in calamity.

For their formal initiation as rulers, they likely complete the Sea King's Recitation of Vows:

NO EXPLORING SUNKEN SHIPS.

NO INTERACTING WITH HUMANS.

NO MISSING ANY GATHERING
OF ANY SORT.

All these rules make me uneasy. Maybe that's because Mother expects me to follow so many royal rules. I just can't do it. Maybe I wasn't cut out for island royalty after all.

THE
SEA KING

While many old tales describe how merfolk
rulers take and leave their thrones in waters
around the world, one thing remains constant
in every legend: the Sea King rules over all
merfolk. Almighty, he manages all comings
and goings, oversees all correspondence, and
ensures that order is maintained in all oceans
at all times. . . . These next few pages strive to
illuminate the living legend as old as the briny
sea itself. . . .

LEGEND
OF THE
SEA KING

With talk of merpeople fresh on my tongue, I happened upon a town in Peruvia where locals spoke of the Sea God: a merman who rules all oceans with his powerful pronged scepter and mighty conch shell. Father to the seven rulers of the Seven Seas, he is rumored to have existed for as long as anyone can recall, the same sovereign present at the time of the Fateful Rift between humans and merfolk.

Legend has it that the Sea God now stays concealed in a grand undersea palace, preventing merfolk from swimming to the world above to meddle with humans. He is a strong and powerful merman who protects his underwater realm from all manner of threats. To that end, he is also said to have special gifts of controlling water and wave, lightning and storm cloud.

Crown

Trident

Conch

STORMS OF THE SEA KING

Heave ho!

On a day when the sea was storm tossed and wind whipped, with towering waves and troughs like valleys, I wondered if it might be the Sea King churning a great typhoon as a punishment for all those aboard who'd ever pierced his waves with spears and cut his crests with nets, setting their shrouds to shuddering and flooding the quarterdeck with thieving swells to drag men overboard.

I hid in the captain's cabin, holding on for dear life until, at long last, the storm passed.

Batten down the hatches and crates and it should be all right.
It's probably just a squall coming in, not the work of the Sea God.
Everyone always wants to blame him for anything unpleasant.

Don't tell Mother I think that, though.

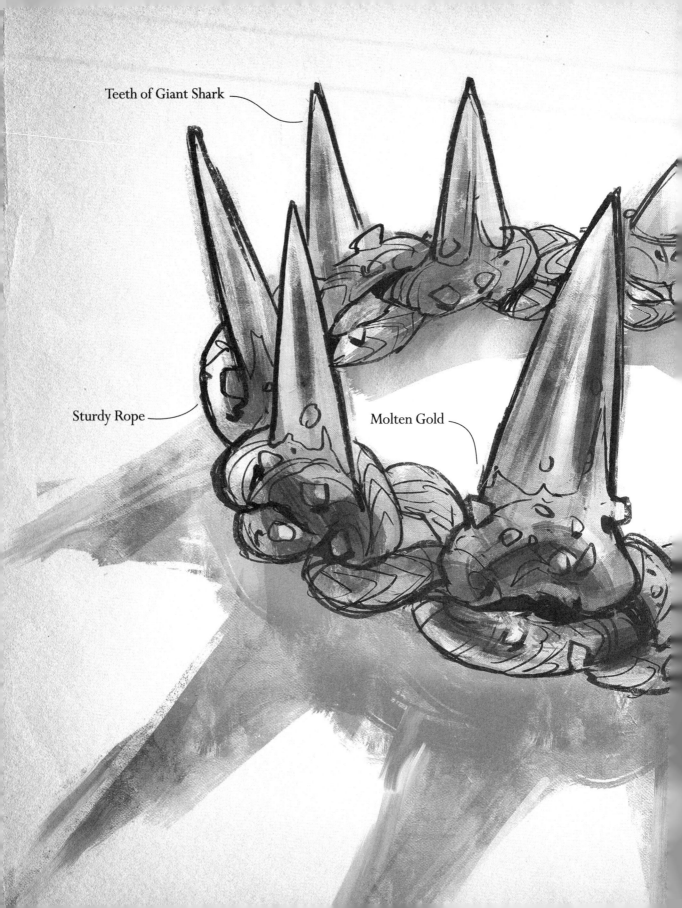

Teeth of Giant Shark

Sturdy Rope

Molten Gold

THE SEA KING'S CROWN

The Sea King's crown is a wreath of legend. Said to be crafted from the gigantic serrated teeth of a shark, forged in molten gold in an undersea volcano, and tied with unbreakable twine, the crown is a symbol of power and might, and is worn proudly by the Sea King, who strikes an intimidating figure even in the siltiest of waters. The shiny diadem is said to garner respect amongst the merfolk, prompting solemn bows of reverence in his presence.

According to legend, the Sea King plucked out the giant shark's teeth with his bare hands, suffering not so much as a scratch, after the shark threatened to eat his seven daughters in their clam beds. After this, he was venerated as a hero among his merpeople.

THE SEA KING'S TRIDENT

Described throughout ancient texts as a shimmering gold staff ending in three prongs, the Sea King's trident is his primary power conduit and weapon of renown, which signifies his rank as ruler of all undersea realms. The trident is passed down from ruler to ruler and has been in the Sea King's clutches for more eons than anyone cares to remember. The shiny, sleek staff maintains the natural order, and, with a flourish, the Sea King can command the oceanic elements, from mists, riptides, and undertows to punishing waves. Other names the trident goes by are Storm Stirrer, Sky Skewer, Water Wand, and Sea Spire.

WHIRLPOOLS

The swift rotation of trident in hand forms a sucking funnel devouring all within its ruinous reach.

STORM

When aimed skyward, the trident summons great and terrible storms.

RAIN

One twist of the trident sunders the skies
and pelts all below with torrents of rain.

*Rosa always blames the Sea King for downpours.
Maybe she's been right all along.*

LIGHTNING

A wave and a twirl of the trifurcated staff
send lightning branching across a black sky.

— POWERS OF THE TRIDENT —

— *three sharp prongs*

— *tines forged in volcanic vents*

— *untarnished gold*

— *ability to shrink and grow wielder to extreme proportions (?)*

— *ability to turn a merperson into a human (??)*

— *used for throwing or dueling (???)*

THE UNDERWATER PALACE

According to the legends, the palace is a grand dwelling on the seafloor, a sprawling place built of shell and limestone, with coral lawns and roofs festooned with clamshells, crystals, and pearls. It is also rumored to be home of the Sea King, along with his royal advisor, royal guards, and merfolk of high status from near and far.

Rumors of the Sea King's palace describe it as a place where he and his court have met for official gatherings over hundreds of years. Most stories say that it is in the Carinae Sea, and that it is the most ornate and most colorful castle ever seen, with sparkling turrets and towers.

I can't believe such amazing things exist down there, but . . . I do.

THE THRONE ROOM

After much research into the many tales of the Sea King and his kingdom, my findings are as follows: the palace has a main space used strictly to hold meetings and host guests. This is called the Throne Room. Here, the Sea King holds court and presides over grand gatherings and ceremonies. The hall, perhaps more of a cave or elevated coral theater, has a floor of sand and coral, with sunlight streaming down. The Sea God sits on his throne overlooking his audience, such as his seven daughters arranged in a circle, each resting her fins on a lifted ledge of coral.

THE ROYAL GUARD

Contingents of soldiers stationed outside and inside the Undersea Palace are said to protect royal members and commoners of the kingdom from any and all threats. Armed with spears and staves, maces and shell-bone daggers, the guards swim circles around the palace and defend it from all manner of danger. The unmatched power of the Sea King's trident is desired by many, warranting a great number of guards to ensure its safekeeping as well as the continued well-being of the king.

And here I was thinking Max was a fearsome guard. Ha!

THE ROYAL ADVISOR

Legends recall that the Sea King has a royal advisor officially appointed by the monarch himself to serve as liaison to a great many. The royal advisor delivers reports of the goings-on in the kingdom, collects information, and communicates to various factions of the kingdom on behalf of the King. The royal advisor is usually a small undersea creature, like a seahorse or an octopus, and recent accounts seem to agree that the current royal advisor is a red crab.

OCTOPUS

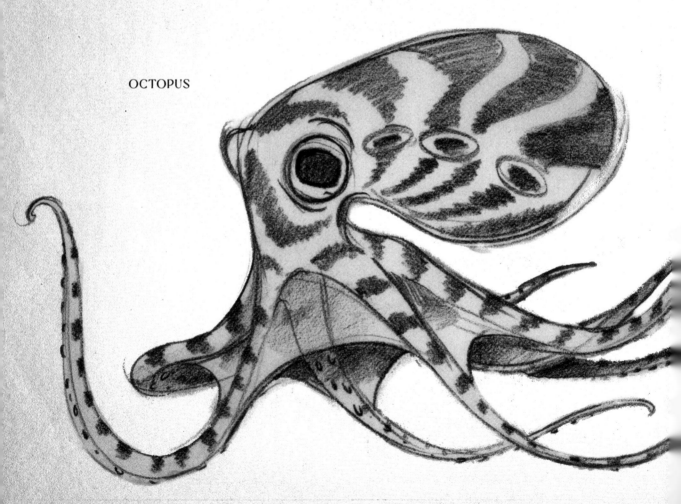

CRAB

I've always said a crab could do Grimsby's job!
That old crabapple. I really hope he isn't reading this right now.
If so, I love you, Grim! Now step away from the book.

SEAHORSE

TRAGEDY OF THE MERMAID QUEEN

Crossing the Carinae Sea, I came upon a report about the Sea Queen, the wife of the Sea King and mother of their seven daughters. According to my findings, she was beloved by merfolk the oceans wide. She used her beautiful singing voice to heal and to mend. It is said that she was taken with humans, that she frequented the surface, visiting humans in hopes of bridging the Ancient Division. The Sea God was wary of her aims to bring unity in the modern age—for humans and merfolk to live in kinship and amity once again. But the Sea God was gradually warming to the future she promised to help bring about, until one direful day.

The report said that fifteen years ago, fishers reported disturbances in the water. A merperson beckoned a sailor to the water's edge before trying to drag him under. He escaped, horrorstricken, and called his comrades to his aid. In the weeks that followed, the terror continued, a

haunting over town and boat. The face in the water bore a crown, and all assumed it was the Sea Queen. But they were all deceived, for it was actually a terrible sea witch, disguised in the Sea Queen's likeness by trick of dark magic spell. The Sea Witch antagonized the humans, tipping their boats and tripping their legs, and sailors began to disappear. One day, the Sea Witch tried to capsize a boat in the harbor, but the humans had grown savvy and trapped her in a large net.

The true Sea Queen heard the thrashing fracas above and sped to the Sea Witch's rescue, freeing her from the net. She begged the Sea Witch to retreat into the depths with her, but the Sea Witch was enraged at those who had dared ensnare her. She gnashed her teeth, circling the boat, and lashing out at its hull. The men would have no more of it. One wielded a harpoon and sent it sailing through the air toward the Sea Witch. The rusted barbs struck with a killing blow—but the men had gotten it wrong, and the harpoon had taken that life of the real, innocent Sea Queen instead. The Sea Witch slipped away unscathed, ruthless, and glad to have escaped with her own life.

The Sea King's grief for his wife grew until he made the decision to forbid any of his merpeople from ever visiting the surface again. He also banished the Sea Witch. Any kindness he had ever shown her was gone, and any fondness he had begun to feel for humans went away after that doomful day as well, eclipsed once more by his great dislike for us all. . . .

What a tragic end. This is exactly why I condemn my crew whenever they're champing at the bit to send a harpoon flying at the first flash of movement. Never know when it could be an innocent mermaid down there, or a dolphin! I'm always telling my mates to use their eyes and their senses.

THE SEVEN SEAS

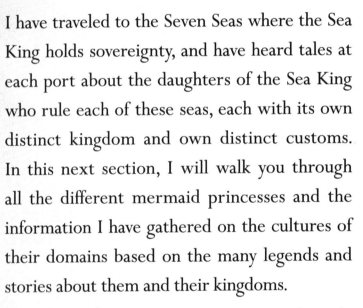

I have traveled to the Seven Seas where the Sea King holds sovereignty, and have heard tales at each port about the daughters of the Sea King who rule each of these seas, each with its own distinct kingdom and own distinct customs. In this next section, I will walk you through all the different mermaid princesses and the information I have gathered on the cultures of their domains based on the many legends and stories about them and their kingdoms.

This explorer has got me beat when it comes to travel. At least for now.

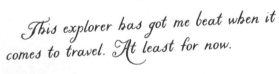

RULERS OF THE SEVEN KINGDOMS

I have compiled all the information I could gather about each reigning sister on the pages that follow after crossing the globe and back. . . . Each princess rules one of the great Seven Kingdoms.

It has been contested amongst scholars on schooners whether the seven daughters of the Sea King are mermaids or sirens. Some think they are sirens because of how much power each is said to possess. Others believe they are mermaids because of how kind and non-deadly they are portrayed to be in stories. Though inconclusive, the consensus seems to be that these seven rulers are powerful mermaids who are beloved by their father, the Sea King.

CASPIA

MALA

INDIRA

TAMIKA

KARINA

PERLA

ARIEL

I can't wait to learn about life in each undersea kingdom.
I really admire how the author reached out to other cultures
to learn about their stories. It's important to stay connected
with the rest of the world so we don't get left behind. On my
next trip, I'm hoping to trade our sugar cane for quinine.
Fun Fact: Quinine is used in Euporia to cure malaria!

PRINCESS MALA
RULER OF THE CHAINE SEA

Princess Mala is the fierce ruler of the Chaine Sea. Legends claim that she is the most fearless of all her sisters, committed to protecting her reefs at all costs. She detests shipwrecks lest they ruin her ocean, and fights back a toxic red tide that plagues her shores.

THE CHAINE SEA

The Chaine Sea is south of the Chiveil mainland. The waters are full of islands, shoals, and cays. Princess Mala rules over all those living in the Chaine Sea and its connecting rivers.

MALA'S RULING STYLE

Princess Mala is reportedly a strong and intrepid leader and is beloved for her sense of humor. She is rumored in one popular tale to have once sent messages on scrolls of seaweed to humans through the courier service of great crested terns before her father banned further interactions.

I wish that were still a thing!

CHAINE SEA MARINE LIFE

◄ BAIJI ►

◄ SEA TURTLE ►

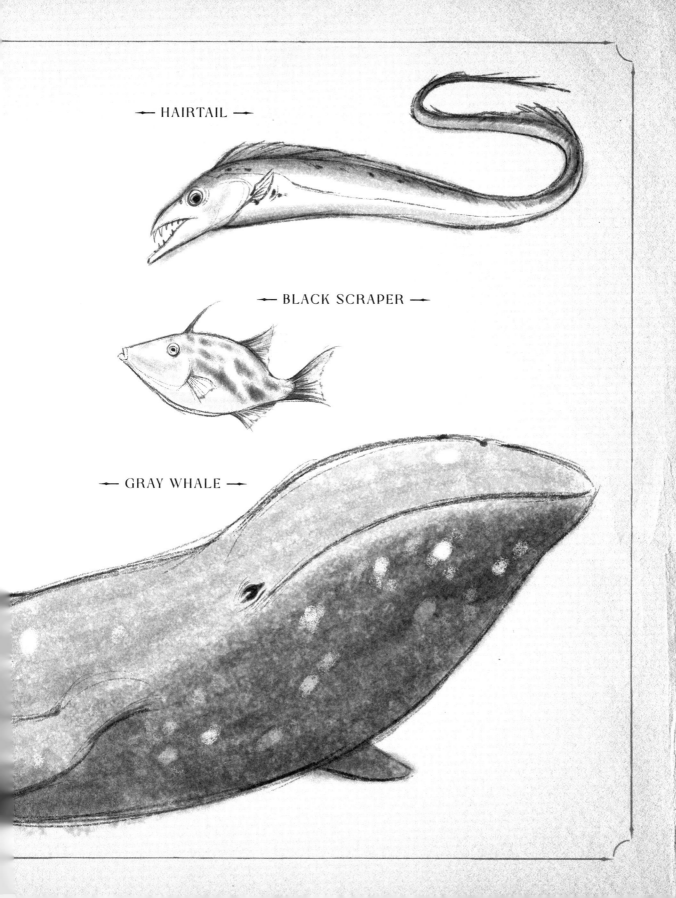

HAIRTAIL

BLACK SCRAPER

GRAY WHALE

ENVIRONMENT
OF THE CHAINE SEA

On my voyage across the Chaine Sea, a topographer on board claimed the bottom of the Chaine Sea was rife with troughs and seamounts, coral reefs and fields of seagrass. It is believed that merfolk tend the grass fields. The roots of trees in the mangrove forests are used by the merfolk to house outlaws and criminals. It is said that the merfolk in the Chaine Sea sleep soundly in algal beds and giant clams after consuming calming cups of squid-ink tea.

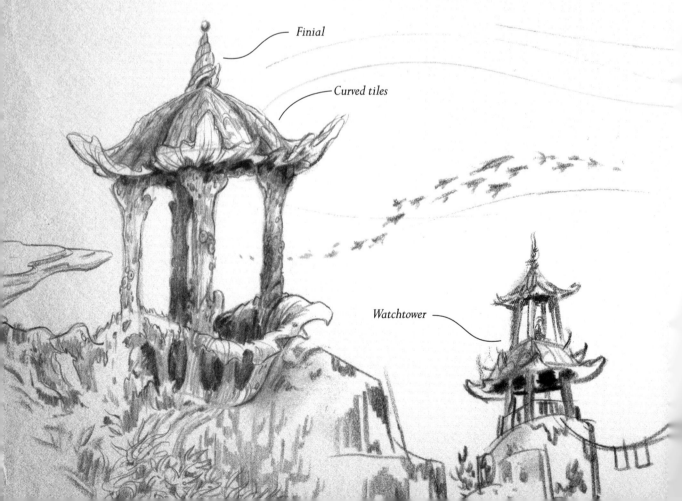

Finial

Curved tiles

Watchtower

KINGDOM OF CHAINE

Tiered tower

Crest with clam carving holding pearl

Main building

Column

Steps

CULTURE
OF THE CHAINE SEA

Stories claim that merfolk in the Chaine Sea are skilled at opera and acrobatics. They celebrate mid-autumn by spending time with family, and laud the start of spring by riding seahorses. They host the festivals of the Sponge Moon, where merfolk revitalize their spirits, and the Salmon Sun, for renewal. Princess Mala commands and listens to her subjects from inside her watchtower.

Legends say that in the kingdom of Chaine, merfolk greet one another by bowing into a somersaulting loop. Blowing bubbles is considered a sign of gratefulness, while pointing one's tail at another is deemed inconsiderate. On holidays, the merfolk sing opera while wearing coral jewelry. They tend to end any event with a meal of fresh clams.

PRINCESS TAMIKA

RULER OF THE FRACUS SEA

Princess Tamika is the mighty ruler of the Fracus Sea. Legends describe her as the most tactical of all her sisters, ruling with an iron fin.

Some say she once wrestled a tiger shark into submission before it swam off.

Incredible!

THE FRACUS SEA

The Fracus Sea is between Frican and Saas, and meets with the Dianian Ocean. The clear, sunlit waters brim with vibrant fish and coral. Princess Tamika rules everyone living in the Fracus Sea.

TAMIKA'S RULING STYLE

In many old books, writers say that Princess Tamika leads her kingdom with admirable strength and grace. She is a fierce ruler as well as mighty warrior, trained in hand-to-fin combat. She is as wise as she is strong, reigning over sprawling reefs, and is very knowledgeable about currents and winds.

FRACUS SEA MARINE LIFE

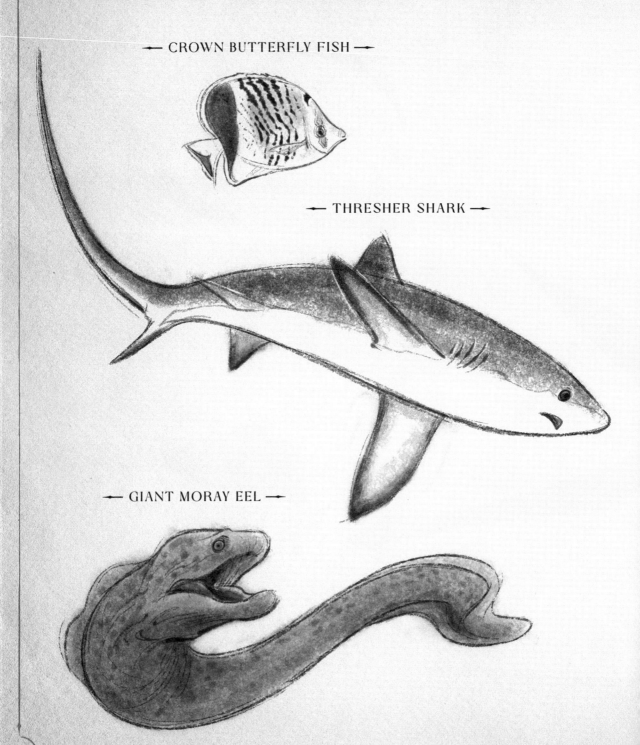

→ CROWN BUTTERFLY FISH →

→ THRESHER SHARK →

→ GIANT MORAY EEL →

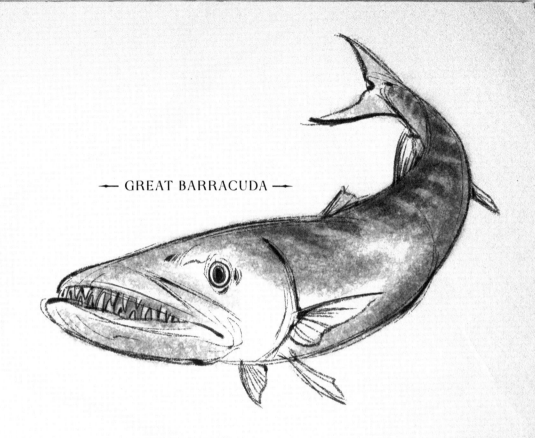

← GREAT BARRACUDA →

← LIONFISH →

ENVIRONMENT
OF THE FRACUS SEA

Scholars believe that Princess Tamika's palace sits in the center of an extravagant coral city bustling with vivid fish. The palace, along with all structures on the floor of the Fracus Sea, is built into the coral. The city limits end at a drop-off into the depths. This is called the Coral Wall, which is guarded by merfolk with the aim of keeping trouble at bay. At night, the city lights up with glowing coral.

Pinnacle

KINGDOM OF FRACUS

Bulbous dome

CULTURE
OF THE FRACUS SEA

In legends, the merfolk in the Fracus Sea are known for using their environment to fashion unique objects, like javelins created from sharpened coral that they throw into looped targets for sport. Gift giving is highly valued in this undersea community. They host the gatherings of the Fluke Moon, when merfolk hang decorative ornaments on wire coral, and the Lamprey Sun, when merfolk join hands at sunset to make their shadow below resemble the sun.

In the kingdom of Fracus, merfolk greet each other by wrapping a current of water around one another in a sort of aquatic embrace. A gift should be refused nine times before it is accepted, and compliments should always be met with modesty. On holidays, the merfolk eat oyster stew, then chant while planting kelp on great stone monoliths on the seafloor.

PRINCESS KARINA
RULER OF THE SAITHE SEA

Princess Karina is the tailstrong ruler of the Saithe Sea, otherwise known as the Dark Sea.

Rumor is that she is the most decisive of all her sisters, with strong intuition.

Stories depict her as very fearful of humans, and many tales describe her protecting harp seals against them.

Poor harp seals.

THE SAITHE SEA
The Saithe Sea is off the northwest coast of Otrax. The waters are typically coated in ice. Princess Karina presides over merfolk, fish, and creatures dwelling in the Saithe Sea.

KARINA'S RULING STYLE
Legends say that Princess Karina is the most reclusive of the Sea King's daughters. She is rumored to be very gifted with animals, and she often works closely with the creatures native to her land to make decisions that benefit all of the beings in her domain.

SAITHE SEA MARINE LIFE

← TALANTIC SALMON →

← BOWHEAD →

HARP SEAL

WOLFFISH

WATER NOKK

ENVIRONMENT
OF THE SAITHE SEA

The ice-covered waters below a pale northern sky hide many secrets in their frigid depths, protecting those beneath from prying human eyes— and ice picks. The realm beneath the thick layer of ice is dark and dim, with green water and a jagged seafloor. Accounts claim that most merfolk live in a hollow in the seabed, while those of higher social status, including Princess Karina, dwell in a grand city carved beneath a floating iceberg. When one iceberg melts, the merfolk carve a city into the next largest. At night, comb jellies light up the city.

Unbelievable . . .

Ice palace arched entrance (detail)

Intricate patterns

KINGDOM OF SAITHE

Main structure of iceberg

*Immaculate.
But I still wouldn't
be caught dead in
such freezing-cold
waters.*

CULTURE
OF THE SAITHE SEA

According to many texts, those in the Saithe Sea used to poke their heads up through holes in the ice to converse with humans. Sometimes, it's said, they'd rejoice underwater as snow fell from the hole in the ice. Ever since visits to the surface were forbidden, the merfolk have kept to the misty waters. Stories say they are skilled at ballet and at tending to sea anemone gardens. Superstitions include a sea angel alighting on one's palm taken to mean good fortune, and it is traditional to collect stacks of perfectly nesting shells. They host the celebration of the Chub Moon as well as the Slug Sun Festival, where merfolk chase a rare and rapid Fire Fish, which sheds one lucky wishing scale to the competition's victor.

Legends say that merfolk in the kingdom of Saithe greet one another by kissing each other six times on the cheek, alternating sides. Whistling is considered discourteous, and a pessimistic outlook on life is strongly discouraged. On holidays, after a feast of shellfish, the merfolk dance below a sheet of ice shimmering with the lights from the aurora borealis, while young ones carve artful and fantastical shapes with shells on the underside of the ice to show off to their esteemed elders.

I wonder what I'd wish for. . . .

PRINCESS INDIRA
RULER OF THE BRINEDIVE SEA

Princess Indira is the gentle ruler of the Brinedive Sea. Rumor is that she is the most generous of all her sisters, leading with empathy and kindness.

One common legend says that she saved her subjects from a rampaging giant venomous sea snake.

THE BRINEDIVE SEA

The Brinedive Sea is located between Diani and the Brinedive Peninsula, and touches the northwest part of the Dianian Ocean. The waters in the gulf are shallow, sunny, and hot. Princess Indira reigns over merfolk as well as fish and creatures dwelling in the Brinedive Sea.

INDIRA'S RULING STYLE

Stories claim that Princess Indira is skilled in diplomacy, working well with the ministers of her court. She is incredibly knowledgeable about her ocean and the other kingdoms, and she is often depicted in books as an excellent debater.

BRINEDIVE SEA MARINE LIFE

← BOTTLENOSE DOLPHIN →

← TUNA →

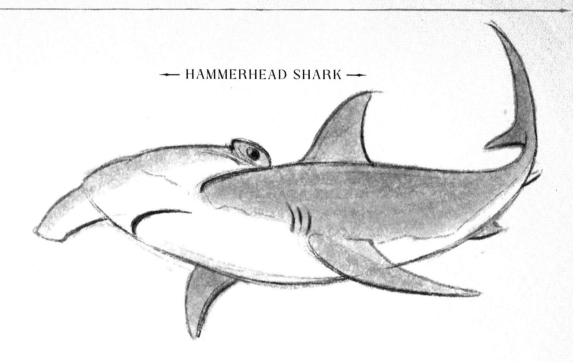

— HAMMERHEAD SHARK —

— MOONFISH —

— SEA CUCUMBER —

ENVIRONMENT
OF THE BRINEDIVE SEA

At first glance, the sunny waters of the Brinedive Sea look deserted, with sandy plains and rocks. However, some think the merpeople live in tunnels and burrows concealed beneath the sand by some form of camouflage. For the longest time, there were reports of merpeople sightings in a calm part of the Brinedive Sea, where they'd bask on small islands and rocks. In other parts, merfolk are said to care for sea turtles at seagrass meadows and pastures, where they protect the grazing sea turtles.

Undersea city

Palace

I once followed a ship of Dianian traders to port on the mainland to see what they'd brought to trade. Cassia and cinnamon! What I'd give to visit the spice traders on the Brinedive Sea.

KINGDOM OF BRINEDIVE

Who knew all this architectural splendor existed down there?!

Onion dome

CULTURE
OF THE
BRINEDIVE SEA

Legends claim that merfolk in the Brinedive Sea create dust clouds by stirring up the seafloor to disorient any threats, such as the white-tipped reef shark or barracuda. The sea fern is sacred to these merfolk, and the cormorant is their eyes above the water. They host the celebration of the Angler Moon, when merfolk decorate a sea fern before taking hold of a passing whale shark and letting it carry them a distance. They also receive merfolk from other realms to huddle into pods for the Ray Sun festival, when they cheer on hatchling sea turtles crawling from shore to sea, shooing off terns and cormorants with their warning songs.

Stories say that merfolk in the kingdom of Brinedive greet one another by shaking fins while maintaining eye contact. All their meals start and end with mussels, which is a mark of hospitality. The largest mussels are typically reserved for guests. On holidays, the merfolk sing whale songs. If they sing well, a whale will hear the song from afar and sing back

PRINCESS CASPIA
RULER OF THE APNEIC SEA

Princess Caspia is the generous ruler of the Apneic Sea. Stories describe her as the most selfless of all her sisters, serving her people first, leading second.

It is said that she is a bit reclusive, traveling only for all-seas gatherings.

THE APNEIC SEA

The Apneic Sea is an inland sea between Euporia and Saas. The waters are brackish and murky, with rocky islands and sometimes ice. Princess Caspia rules over those living in the Apneic Sea.

CASPIA'S RULING STYLE

In the legends, Princess Caspia values knowledge. She is rumored to have created a river that cuts through Diani and connects to the Chaine Sea for visiting other undersea kingdoms. She also is very protective of coral and makes many laws to help ensure that it thrives in her kingdom.

Coral is so important. So many animals make their homes in it.

APNEIC SEA MARINE LIFE

← GREAT STURGEON →

← PIKE →

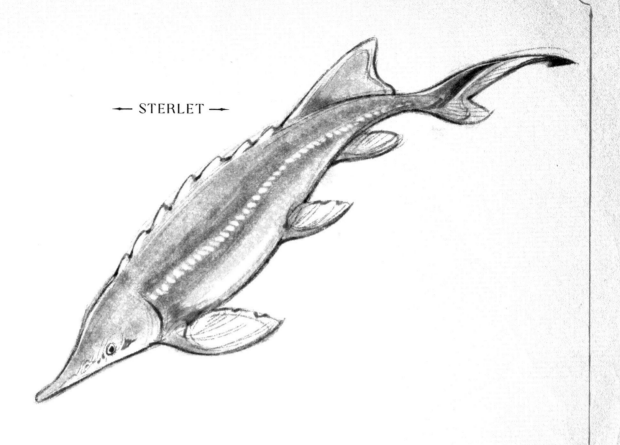

— STERLET —

— CHUB —

ENVIRONMENT OF THE APNEIC SEA

The undersea realm of the Apneic Sea is home to sunken ships that were quickly claimed by the sea, then by those within it. It is said that many merfolk have made their homes inside these ships. Other merfolk settlements and villages have been built into sea cliffs—more specifically, on shelves of shells, with colossal conches for roofs.

In warmer waters, there are remote sand bars and shoals where adolescent merfolk socialize. Scholars believe that merfolk also explore the seamount range and the caverns within or ride giant sturgeons across the plains for sport. There is a depression on the seabed where the water is at its deepest, an abandoned place said to be haunted by ancient, tormented sea spirits.

Shell homes

KINGDOM OF THE APNEIC SEA

Sunken ship

Sea cliffs

CULTURE
OF THE APNEIC SEA

Merfolk in the Apneic Sea are suspected to value punctuality and be highly superstitious. They believe it is bad luck to swim with one's back to another merperson. They tie soft corals together with seagrass to manifest marriage, and even have matchmakers. On the first day of summer, they rub mud on their fins for success. To that same effect, they stay awake the whole night on the first day of winter. For sport, they draw artistic shapes in the sand and practice coral storytelling to regale the young ones with tales of good versus evil.

Merfolk in the kingdom of Apneic are believed to greet one another by brushing scales with each other. At weddings, they throw barnacles at the newly wedded, and when merbabies are born, the caretakers rub a mix of sand and clay onto their foreheads and the tips of their fins. They swim around at night singing arias to lull restless merbabies in the kingdom to sleep in their clam cribs.

PRINCESS PERLA
RULER OF THE PITON SEA

Princess Perla is the steadfast ruler of the Piton Sea. Rumor is that she is the most charismatic of all her sisters, radiating warmth and kindness.

It is said that she once charmed a pod of hungry orcas out of attacking a colony of penguins.

THE PITON SEA

The Piton Sea is just off the Cartograph coast of Gargentine. The waters are temperate and very deep. Princess Perla rules over all those living in the Piton Sea and its connecting rivers.

PERLA'S RULING STYLE

Princess Perla is believed to rule her kingdom with good-naturedness, and is respected by all she governs. She is very thoughtful with her choices as a leader and often puts decisions to a vote to keep the peace.

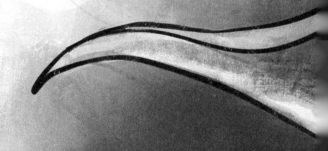

PITON SEA MARINE LIFE

ELEPHANT SEAL

PENGUIN

DUSKY DOLPHIN

SEA OTTER

All this talk of the sea sure is making me miss it.
I'm starting to feel restless, and Mother knows it. The library's quiet.
No one comes in here but me, usually to add to my assortment of
keepsakes or to pore over sailing charts in the candlelight.

ENVIRONMENT
OF THE PITON SEA

Tales describe the underwater landscape of the Piton Sea as having seamounts and canyons (troughs), but most notably towering kelp forests. The sun filtering through these forests' canopies casts all of Perla's kingdom in a soft green light. The Great Kelp Forest provides protection from outsiders, obscuring it from human passersby. There are shanty towns on the outskirts of the kingdom with homes made up of enormous sea urchins, while dwellings closer to the palace consist of large shells with pillars of kelp. Merfolk here travel inconspicuously beneath orca or humpback whale, and the surface is often coated by a frothy layer of sea foam.

Spiral palace

KINGDOM OF THE PITON SEA

Coral pathways

Shell structures

CULTURE
OF THE PITON SEA

It is said that merfolk in the Piton Sea ride elephant seals for sport and value music played on instruments such as shell-filled maracas. They also enjoy playing hide-and-seek in the kelp, kelp-twirling, and kelp-dancing, a form of aquatic dance akin to the art of human silk aerialists. They host the celebration of the Clam Moon, where merfolk race each other through hoops under its wan light, as well as the Sprat Sun festival.

In the kingdom of Piton, when merfolk meet for the first time, stories say one sings a sequence of notes, and the other echoes them back, adding a single note to the end of the original sequence. Nodding at one another is considered friendly. A popular dish is sea urchins wrapped in seaweed. On special occasions, the merfolk take turns singing tales of long-gone ancestors.

PRINCESS ARIEL
RULER OF THE CARINAE SEA

That's my sea!

Princess Ariel is the spirited ruler of the Carinae Sea. Legends say that she is the most sensitive of all her sisters, with a loving, tender heart.

Rumor is that she has a fascination with the human world, collecting human trinkets from sunken ships.

THE CARINAE SEA

The Carinae Sea is off the north coast of South Ustelo. The waters are warm and crystal clear. Princess Ariel rules over all those living in the Carinae Sea.

ARIEL'S RULING STYLE

Princess Ariel is said to rule her kingdom with an endearing kindness, and is beloved by all. In stories, Princess Ariel is revered for her remarkable singing voice and curiosity. She believes in the power of togetherness and unity, and she has a gift for seeing the best in her people.

Princess Ariel . . .
She reminds me of my little jade mermaid.

CARINAE SEA MARINE LIFE

— GREAT WHITE SHARK —

— MANATEE —

◄ BLOWFISH ►

◄ CRAB ►

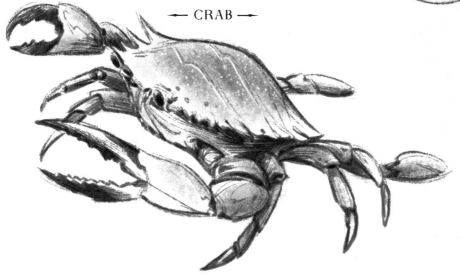

◄ POWDER BLUE TANG ►

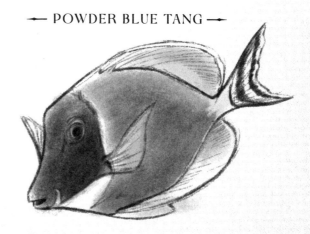

*I'm pretty sure I've seen all these
creatures swimming in the clear blue.*

ENVIRONMENT
OF THE CARINAE SEA

The Carinae Sea is said to be the home to the great Palace of the Sea King. Ariel is rumored to live within a tower in the East Wing of the palace. The city sprawled below the palace is a landscape of limestone homes fashioned with shells and clams, as well as meadows where herds of sea cows are raised.

This is a realm of earthquakes, tsunamis, and trenches deeper down where volcanoes rumble and flow. Parts of the sea lead into estuaries and lagoons. Coral is aplenty, as the Carinae Sea is also where Merman's Reef can be found, as well as the Shipwreck Graveyard, which is said to be cursed with huge Great White Sharks.

Legends claim the Sea Witch also doesn't live far from the Sea King's Palace, despite its extremely dark depths. . . .

How interesting . . . It looks so different from how I imagined. . . . All that wonderful culture we humans know so very little about . . .

Pillars

KINGDOM OF THE CARINAE SEA

Coral dome

Palace

CULTURE
OF THE
CARINAE SEA

It is believed that merfolk in the Carinae Sea play games of sea cricket and celebrate the birthday of the Sea King by throwing a carnival of music and revelry. Festivals and street fairs, when food vendors line the sandy avenues in a great market, are a common occurrence. Merfolk sing door-to-door to foster merriment. They host the gatherings of the Coral Moon, where merfolk come together to reunite as family, and the Smelt Sun, where ancestors are remembered and honored.

Many scholars claim that merfolk in the kingdom of Carinae greet one another by singing a simple harmony together. Families commonly attend concerts to enjoy merpeople singing onstage with a full orchestra of fish and crustaceans. An outlook of optimism is widely applauded. A popular dish consists of seaweed seasoned with various herbs found growing in sea gardens.

It is said that certain merfolk travel to the trenches to visit the Sea Witch, asking her to put hexes on their enemies. . . .

All that culture and tradition exists right below the surface?
This only makes me want to explore the sea outside even more!

THE
SEA
WITCH

Now that you know about the legends surrounding the Sea King and his daughters, there is one more important sea creature that stories tell of: the Sea Witch. For antagonizing humans and contributing to the unjust demise of the Sea Queen, the Sea King banished this cruel being from his kingdom for the past fifteen years. Stories claim that her place of exile is in the darkness of the deep sea, in a lair full of rage and hate fueled further by her ostracism. No longer is she a citizen of the Seven Seas. She is a feared and wicked figure in legends.

I felt the Sea Witch worthy of her own section, to illuminate the intricacies of her story. . . .

Okay, she sounds like pure evil.
I would not want to cross her path!

THE LORE
OF THE
SEA WITCH

Rumor is that the Sea Witch grew up in a palace, enjoying lavish feasts and celebrations until her exile after antagonizing humans resulted in the Sea Queen's demise (see page 98). A master of potions, elixirs, poultices, and spells, she is most known for her dealmaking, in which she utilizes unbreakable contracts to bind other merfolk to inescapable circumstances in exchange for her own desires.

Her most well-known goal is to get her hands on the Sea King's almighty trident once more, and with it, to undo the Sea King and to rule the Seven Seas, bending merperson and human to her most wicked will.

Legend claims that in the farthest depths of the ocean, past volcanic eruptions and darkest abysses, she dwells in her sinister lair: banished, ostracized, and vengeful, with an inky black heart.

But this pariah, like most merfolk, was born with a gift, a special magic all her own. . . .

Something about this seems foreboding. . . .

ANATOMY OF THE SEA WITCH

This is truly terrifying.

Plume of white hair

Shell earrings

Shell necklace

Tentacle

Suckers

Unlike other merpeople the Sea Witch is said to be a species all her own: half human (the upper half), half octopus (the lower half).

THE LAIR
OF THE SEA WITCH

In lore, the Sea Witch inhabits twisted caves tunneled beneath the skeletal remains of a bony prehistoric whale. Through dark winding corridors lies the heart of her lair. Legend says her home is built from the skulls and bones of shipwrecked humans. There, she sits in a giant blue pearlescent clamshell throne on a rock ledge. Below it stands a pedestal with glowing red contracts atop it. The obsidian lair is completely dark save for a small stream of light from an opening above. Her cronies present themselves as two thick gray eels with sharp teeth. Each has a single gold-glowing eye. They wind around her arms like a shawl and slither about her room. It's said she has cages of coral and shells that hold shrimp for consuming.

I don't remember seeing "eel" as an option for Common Merfolk Companions. Well, it suits her!

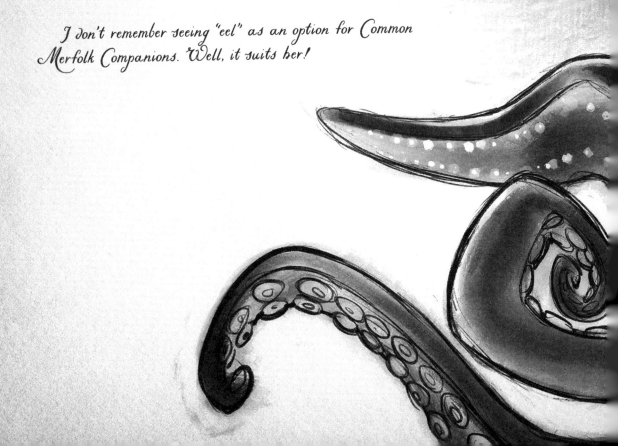

THE CLAMSHELL THRONE

That's the largest clamshell I've ever imagined!

The Giant Clamshell functions as throne to the SeaWitch,
who occupies it while scheming. . . .

THE BLACK PEARL

Many stories describe the Sea Witch using an obsidian-black pearl to gaze at visions of past, present, and future. Legend says that her pet eels have a sacred connection to this large pearl: what they see in the present moment can be projected as images inside the pearl's clarifying sphere for the Sea Witch to witness from the safety of her lair. In this way, the eels act as her eyes. The Black Pearl floats within an enormous opened oyster shell.

Maybe Mother was right about merpeople. Maybe there is much to fear. . . .

DEALS OF THE SEA WITCH

When merpeople grow desperate in life, rumor is that they sometimes resort to diving down to the Sea Witch's lair in secret to barter with her: her magic spells in exchange for something the Sea Witch desires. The merfolk come to her in flocks, pleading for love spells, for the ability to transform into humans, for power and riches beyond compare. But with the Sea Witch, there is always a catch. A heavy price, a high demand, a sacrifice that the needy merfolk must make if they do not follow through with their end of the bargain.

INCANTATIONS

Scholars report that the Sea Witch has committed to memory a repertoire of incantations that help her make her deals, learned from trial and tribulations over her years living in solitude and practicing her magic gift.

POTIONS AND ELIXIRS

She also concocts various brews, which she corks in vials and ensconces in glass spheres, then racks.

— ground tusk of walrus
— whisker of seal
— molar of dugong
— sludge of trench
— bone from the abyss
— mucus of eel
— barb of stingray
— head of cod
— sea worm
— fish guts and coils
— tongue of tarpon
— butterfly (living)

CONTRACTS AND SCALES

Before the Sea Witch proceeds with any deal for a hopeless soul, she makes the merperson donate a scale plucked from their own tail. Once the scale is tossed into the witch's cauldron with the spell cast, the deal is irreversible, the merperson forever indebted to the Sea Witch.

Grim is always telling me to read the fine print!

NOTABLE SEA WITCH SPELLS

For each deal struck and sealed, the Sea Witch must likely have an accompanying spell to recite upon combining all her ingredients. In my travels, I came upon a merchant who claimed to have found a message in a bottle washed ashore with a list of spells believed to belong to the Sea Witch. After scrupulously poring over them, I have chosen to include my findings to demonstrate the scope of her power. With each pact of the witch, I've gleaned that there is always the want, the take, and the rule to break.

These unbreakable vows seem like bad news. . . .

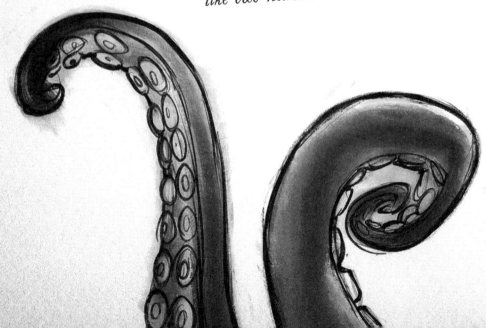

YEARNING SPELL

The Want: To enchant the heart of another for a merperson to grasp love requited

The Take: In exchange for the eyesight of the merperson

The Rule to Break: Before the moon sets on the third night, the merperson must marry their bewitched before an audience of no fewer than ten merpeople without one objection.

INCANTATION

Porpoise Amorphus
Churn foams of the Chaine Sea
Strabismix glaucomis
Et max cataractis
La vista to me

TRANSFORMATION SPELL

The Want: To transform a merperson into a human

The Take: In exchange for the voice of the merperson

The Rule to Break: Before the sun sets on the third day, a human must fall in love with the merperson and give them true love's kiss.

INCANTATION

Beluga Akuba
Blow airs of the Apneic Sea
Aphonix leukplakis
Et max pharyngitis
Il suono from thee

MUSIC SPELL

The Want: To give a merperson the most perfect and powerful singing voice of them all

The Take: In exchange for the hearing of the merperson

The Rule to Break: Before the sun rises on the second day, the merperson must become the official prima donna of their pod.

INCANTATION

Barracuda Sarcuvka
Flow tides of the calm Fracus Sea
Otitis Externis
Et max anakusis
Il udito to me

BEAUTY SPELL

The Want: To make a merperson beautiful through altering physique and face

The Take: In exchange for the personality of the merperson

The Rule to Break: Before the sun sets on the fifth day, the merperson must befriend a new soul with an official fin shake of true friendship.

INCANTATION

Manatee Yamikee
Come cool waves of Carinae Sea
Vitalitis identitis
Et max depressisis
La luce interna to me

POLYP

Legends tell that when merpeople fail to uphold their end of an agreement with the Sea Witch, they belong to her for all eternity and meet a miserable, fearful fate when she turns them into polyps. . . .

These poor unfortunate souls!

The crafty and clever Sea Witch sets up most to fail when it comes to her dubious dealings.

If a merperson does not uphold their end of the agreement, she turns them into a small, withered creature called a polyp, half human, half plant. Legend has it that she used to change her victims into foam, seaweed, and even shrimp, but found the powerless polyp the cruelest and most favored punishment.

The Sea Witch keeps these helpless, harmless souls in a polyp garden that lines the dark nooks and crannies of her dank lair. The colony of polyps moves as one like a bed of horrifying seagrass, each polyp with a haggard maw incapable of uttering a single word, and sad and vacant eyes. They remain in her garden for all time.

Well, just because there's one bad merperson down there doesn't mean all the rest of them are worth fearing. On the whole, I believe that merpeople are more people than they are fish, with beating hearts, hopes, and dreams.

THE
LEGENDS
OF
MERFOLK

This final section tells the tales that merpeople repeat to one another to keep from swimming to surface or shore, and the stories humans tell one another to keep from conspiring with merpeople. These fables I have gathered from my trip around the world and have reproduced on the next several pages. . . .

This should be good! I always hear Lashana and Rosa whispering about these legends in the castle halls when they're folding linens or scrubbing the floors.

THE LEGEND
OF THE
SEA GLASS

One day in the heat of the South Pasifta, a young woman went for a refreshing dip. She swam to a rock out in the bay. Suddenly she saw fins churn the surface. Three enormous sharks began to circle her.

Just then, she felt rough hands take her by the waist, and she was pulled under the water. The next thing she knew, she was being dragged onto the shore. Spluttering, she saw someone beside her: a merman with an orange tail and silky white hair. The merman had saved her from certain death! The young woman thanked the merman, who offered her a piece of green sea glass, sharing that it could create an elixir for everlasting life, and asking the human to keep it safe for him. She agreed. With that, the merman vanished back into the blue.

The next day, hardship and blight struck the island. Plants shriveled up. Coconut meat turned to black rot. And the villagers took ill. She was fearful she would be next. So she ground up the sea glass and devoured it. That way, even if she caught ill, she would survive.

Morning came, finding the young woman well. She set out on her boat, but a storm struck, sending her into a sea cave, where a rockslide trapped her in the gloom. In a clear green puddle on the cave floor, the merman's face appeared. The young woman begged to be rescued, but the merman was furious with her for consuming the sea glass and left her alone.

Having everlasting life meant she could never die, so there she remains, stuck for all time.

Whoa! I wonder if that's true.

THE TALE
OF THE
SCALE

Once, there lived a mermaid who did not like her tail.

It was green like the brackish water in the lagoon and mottled like the sand and silt below. Her friends constantly told her that her tail was beautiful just the way it was. But as they gabbed and giggled on the rocks in a cove alive with the rush of waterfalls, the mermaid sighed, crestfallen, in her hidden self-disgust. If only her tail were pink, or orange, or yellow . . .

One day she was swimming beyond the rocks when a crocodile appeared with enormous jaws and hungry eyes. It began to chase her through the water. Luckily, the coloring of her tail allowed her to blend in with the sand and silt at the bottom of the green lagoon. After watching the crocodile wind through the water above her, she moved toward the surface.

The crocodile spotted her then and zipped toward her. But her powerful tail propelled her to safety on a tall rock.

She regarded her tail, grateful for its strength and ashamed at ever having doubting it.

It is said that a scale molted off her tail and floated out to sea.

The one who keeps it will find a lifetime of joy . . . or turn into a merperson.

That would be amazing! Can you imagine?
A human who could transform into a merperson, or a
merperson who could become a human?

THE TALE
OF THE TREACHEROUS
TIDE POOL

There's an age-old myth of a mermaid who always thought very highly of herself. Her siblings often chided her for being vain, or for looking down her nose at them. But the mermaid did not know for sure if she was beautiful, because there was nothing in which she could gaze at her reflection. One day, a lobster whom she trusted dearly heard of her secret wish, and told her of a place where she would be able to see her reflection: above the surface, where the sand met the sea, there was a cluster of rocks, and just beyond that, she would find what she sought.

The mermaid waited until the moment was right and followed her lobster friend's directions. At the shore, she pulled herself out of the water and crawled across the top of a broad boulder. There, below it, sparkled a tide pool where she could see her face clearly for the first time. She was more beautiful than she had ever imagined, with eyes like the most lustrous pearls and lips as red as brightest fire coral. She sat there for the longest time, admiring her reflection. Soon the sun was at its zenith, the water in the tide pool was dissipating, and the mermaid had grown cracked and dry. Time passed, and the mermaid grew withered. Before long, she was too weak and frail to move from the pool. She stared at her reflection, her eyes never leaving it, and kept doing so until she turned to nothing more than sea foam.

Lashana used to tell me this tale whenever I looked too long in the mirror during fittings as a boy. Little did she know I was daydreaming of the sea.

THE CURSED SAND DOLLAR

On the night of the Coral Moon, as merfolk gathered to celebrate its shining phase, a merman swam alone, languishing in his solitude. Eventually, he came upon a silver sand dollar twinkling on the ocean floor. He collected such oddities and took it up. As he swam home, he wished he weren't so lonely. As if by magic, a school of merfolk appeared around him, laughing and talking to him. Overwhelmed by the sudden surge in attention, the merman rushed home. In moments, the merfolk were at his door, pounding at the windows, wanting to be let in. As he studied the curious sand dollar in his hand, he wondered if it was a wishing sand dollar.

He regretted wishing for company, and quickly wished for them to leave him alone.

In moments, the banging and hammering stopped, and the merfolk were gone.

The next day, he entered a great racing competition with a merman of unmatched speed. The prize for the winner consisted of great riches beyond compare. The race began, and the merman secretly used his sand dollar to make a wish. He wished he could be as fast as a sailfish. In moments, the scales on his flipper and fins climbed up his torso, arms, chest, and neck.

The merman's hands turned to fins, which sent the sand dollar slipping from his grasp and falling into the darkness below. When the merman tried to speak, all that escaped his lips was a stream of bubbles. For he had become a fish, and would live the rest of his days as one.

Well, that stinks.

THE ILLUSIONARY TREASURE CHEST

Legend spoke of a treasure chest that merfolk had enchanted in the sea, waiting for the day the most deserving could reach it. One day, a very poor man and his crewmates rowed above a reef. The water was so clear, they could see down to the dappled seafloor below. There, gleaming and glittering, were gold coins and precious gems overflowing from a wooden chest. The men took turns diving through the depths, but the chest was just out of reach when they had to swim up for air. The men returned home, bereft, but told all in the village of the untouchable treasure.

On the dawn of a low tide, the wealthiest man in the village had gotten wind of the precious prize and boasted that he alone could hold his breath long enough to retrieve it. He set out in a boat rowed by the very poor man. At the reef, the wealthy man took a great inhale and plummeted. Within moments, the twinkling treasure chest was within reach. Despite his aching lungs, he moved to grasp the sides of the trunk—and his hands went right through it!

Awestruck, he tried again and again to grab the riches, but his hands and fingers went right through them, as if the chest and all its contents were but a ghost. His lungs screamed for air. Just then, the poor man appeared beside him, grabbed hold of him, and propelled them upward.

Back in the boat, the poor man explained that his concern had filled his lungs with the extraordinary strength to make the deep dive. The wealthy man thanked him, and then something caught his eye: the treasure chest, which the poor man had also somehow brought up. When the wealthy man made to grab it, the poor man lifted the chest and offered it to him: his hands were able to hold it without passing straight through. In that moment, the wealthy man realized the poor man should keep the treasure. In the end, the poor man's noble heart was most deserving indeed.

Lashana used to tell me this one whenever I begged for extra papaya.

LEGEND
OF THE
DAGGER SHELL

Once there lived a fisherman who plagued the waters with his nets and spears. He enmeshed turtles and dolphins, scared off fish, and poured buckets of chum into the sea, clouding its surface. The presence of his boat blotted out the sun over a reef home to a particular siren.

This siren did not want to share her waters with such a nuisance. Her lobster companion had been snared in his trap, and debris filtered through the water from the enormous vessel. But her singing talents were not yet refined, and therefore her siren powers were sadly ineffective. She could not cause the fisherman to fall ill, or capsize his boat, or lure him to his fate.

One day the siren visited the Sea Witch, asking for help to rid the sea of the fisherman. The Sea Witch gave her a dagger-shaped seashell in exchange for her feeble singing voice. One touch of the dagger-shaped seashell to the fisherman's chest would steal his heart. That night, the siren gifted this dagger-shaped seashell to a dear merman friend and tasked him with taking the heart from the scurrilous fisherman to make sure he was dead, for try as she might, she simply could not muster up the resolve to do the dastardly deed herself.

Her friend agreed, for he was hard-bitten and unfeeling. The next day, the loyal merman swam to the surface beside the fisherman's boat and deftly yanked him into the water. But when the merman lifted the dagger shell, poised for the fatal blow, they locked eyes and fell in love.

The merman had taken the fisherman's heart, but not in the way of ruin.

Everybody's heard this old bedtime story.
Rosa thinks it's so romantic.

THE FLUTE OF THE DEEP

There once was a perfect beach frequented by villagers who would swim or paddle out into the gentle, translucent waves. One day, at earliest light, a swimmer entered the water only to be stung by the tentacle of a jellyfish. As the sun rose higher in the sky, the crowds could see that the entire cove teemed with hundreds of jellyfish. Throughout the day, even more jellyfish arrived, and as much as the people had enjoyed the perfect beach, the jellyfish too found a pleasant home in its waters. A villager spoke of a mermaid rumored to play a flute that could lure away any pest. Perhaps if they could find her, she could help them lead the jellyfish out of the cove. . . .

Lo and behold, the mermaid appeared at the shore the next day, her flute gleaming in her hands. She heard the villagers' gripes and vowed to help them so long as they would promise not to fill her waters with boats and rubbish that fluttered down to litter the seafloor. She played her flute as she dove away from the beach, and the jellyfish followed after her in a sluggish trail until not one remained. The villagers rejoiced. They splashed back into the shallows. They paddled back out on their boats. They trawled the waters, caught fish in their nets, and discarded hooks and lines into the sea.

One day the children of the village woke in their beds, hearing an enchanting music. They followed it out into the night as their parents slept on. The children of the village were never seen again, but legend has it that the mermaid was embittered by the broken promise of the people and lured the children away as a punishment.

Like Grim says, our actions have consequences!

THE TALE OF THE GREAT BRINY STORM

Once upon a time, a merman drifted to the banks of a muddy river, where he set eyes on a beautiful woman washing her clothes in the shallows. Using his merman gift, he was able to hear her thoughts, and felt her kindness and warmth seep into his mind. He swam up to her and told her that she was compassionate and courageous, and the woman could see in the merman's oceanic eyes that he too shared those traits.

And so, each day at noon when she came to wash her laundry on the banks, he would visit her, and they would talk, getting to know each other and enjoying each other's company.

One day the woman let slip to a friend that she had fallen in love with a merman. Her friend, though sworn to secrecy, told another person, who told another. Before long, the entire village knew of the clandestine romance between human and merperson. When the woman's family heard of her affection toward the merman, they forbade her from returning to the river.

And so, the next time the merman appeared, he did not see his true love. Nor the next day. He waited for her for long weeks, which turned to months. Had she betrayed him? Abandoned him? He had trusted her. He had loved her. He still did. He would not give up on her.

It was a lonesome afternoon like every other at the sunny riverbanks when an old woman approached him. She explained that merfolk and humans were not allowed to be together. The village had prohibited it.

Anguished, he swam off and wept. The sea sent a great storm to lash shutter and shake eave. From her home, the young woman heard the drumming rain and knew it was her true love sending her a sign. But what was done was done.

Over the years, their romance was all but forgotten, but the sea remembers.

What a tragic tale. They should have been allowed to be together!

THE TALE
OF A THOUSAND
AND ONE SHIPWRECKS

Once upon a time, there was a great war between one continent of people and another continent of people. This war lasted for decades, with each side trying to ruin the other. It culminated in a great battle out on the open ocean. Cannonballs flew. The skies were rent with smoke and fire.

A thousand and one ships crowded the surface, a faceoff of such grand proportions as the sea had never seen.

Down in the murky waters below, the Sea Witch, who still lived at the Sea King's palace, would have none of it. She detested the way the ships above blocked out the sun and the moon; a constant presence of turmoil and distress falling like comets down from above. One day, when a cannonball zipped through the water and nearly struck her, she decided she had had enough. So she snuck into the throne room of her brother and thieved his trident.

With it, she conjured a storm so great that all thousand and one ships were caught in a massive whirlpool and sank to the seafloor.

The war was over, and she was pleased she had made sure of that. Both sides had been villains in her eyes.

But the coral reefs were damaged by all the sunken ships—the price to pay.

When the Sea King discovered what she had done, he seized his trident back from her and told her she could never be trusted with it again. As for the ships, they still remain: in a shipwreck graveyard, a reminder of the war that once was and the might of the magic trident.

That sure is a lot of power to wield.

THE TALE OF THE GREAT SEA FLOOD

A mermaid played a beautiful harp in a sea cave by the shore. Combined with the musicality of her mellifluous string work was the matter of her voice. It was clear as the shallows with as much depth as the open ocean. She plucked her strings and sang her songs, and she was happy.

One evening, as she played in her cave with its entrance obscured by weeping willow, a band of fishermen heard her music and followed it to her. Lost in song, the mermaid did not hear the men creep closer to her, did not hear them whispering instructions, did not see the giant net as it sailed through the air.

The fishermen brought her to the village square, caged in a shallow fountain with her harp. They ordered her to fill their village with the sound of music, and if she did, they would let her go.

One day turned to two, two to three, and the mermaid wilted in her cage, but her voice was an enchanted voice, and could sing and sing without ever going out completely like a flame.

But she was trapped. There was nothing she could do.

What none knew was the captive mermaid was a daughter of the Sea King.

When he found out what had happened to her, he sent a tsunami crashing over the land. The water took his form, and he lifted roof and wall to locate his singing siren. The Sea King grabbed handfuls of land and pulled them down into the sea: retribution for the parts of the sea the fishermen had claimed with their boats and their nets. At long last, he flooded the village square, where he found his daughter. Using his trident, he freed her from her cage, and they swam through the village and back out to sea. Legend has it that the village eventually recovered from the flood, but that the ocean steals a bit of land from the shore year after year as payment for the humans' treachery.

Note to Self: I'm starting to think PEOPLE are the problem here. . . .

She's the same mermaid we designed our ship's carved figurehead after!

UNCHARTED WATERS

Dear reader, if you have come to the end of my book, I thank you for reading my compilation of all there is to know about merpeople and their undersea realms. I hope what you read surprised you, filled you with a sense of wonder, and made you contemplate whether merperson is friend or foe.

In conclusion, my hope is that humans and merpeople may come together one day in peace, as they once did, and foster their relations once more. Of course, Queen Selina will reign as she sees fit. There are more uncharted waters to navigate, and more worlds to see, both above and below the surface. Who knows what other secrets exist? I urge you, dear reader, to explore the world and experience it for yourself. Form your own opinions after gathering as much information as I have.

Until then, happy reading, happy sailing, and happy living.

Mother wanted me to read this book so I would despise merfolk just as much as she does, but it just makes me more interested in them. I want to set sail now more than ever!

There's something out there beckoning me—not just other human cultures from around the world, but also merfolk culture.

Well, then, I suppose it must nearly be time for me to go out there and finally find it.

Wild uncharted waters await!

—Prince Eric